The Brother & Sister Act

ALSO by JOHN R. DOWNES

FICTION

A Few Deadly Friends

Orphan's Song

NON-FICTION

How to Be Irresistible
Through the Power of Persuasion

NonConfrontation Selling

Try Not to Think of an Orange

The Treasure of the Neighborhoods

THE BROTHER

&

SISTER ACT

A TALE OF STAGE, SCREEN, AND ESPIONAGE

John R. Downes

Trafford
PUBLISHING™

Order this book online at www.trafford.com
or email orders@trafford.com

Most Trafford titles are also available at major online book retailers.

Printed in Victoria, BC, Canada.

ISBN: 978-1-4269-0564-3 (soft)
ISBN: 978-1-4269-0565-0 (ebook)

Trafford rev. 11/19/2009

www.trafford.com

North America & international
toll-free: 1 888 232 4444 (USA & Canada)
phone: 250 383 6864 ♦ fax: 812 355 4082

For the men and women who served British Intelligence (MI6) at Bletchley Park in Buckinghamshire, England and the USO during WWII

and

Mike Adolfae, whose inspiration and encouragement made a major impact on this novel. His father, First Lieutenant Herman J. Adolfae, a USAAF C-47 Transport pilot, was shot down and killed over Dunkirk, France on 24 October, 1944.

O dark, dark, dark,
amid the blaze of noon.
MILTON

The business asketh silent secrecy.
SHAKESPEARE

Contents

Chapter One

JULY 1932

DALTON, NEBRASKA

" ... terrible accident... in Hollywood... wake up!"

Twenty-one year old Kenneth Palmer Kroneldt awakened after midnight to the jangling of a bicycle bell and shouting. He peeked through the curtains of his second floor bedroom. A bicycle plopped sideways onto the unpaved street, as a shadowy figure strode to the wooden porch of Zinkgraf's Mercantile and banged on the door.

Kenneth Palmer Kroneldt resembled his late father, Ernest Palmer—not only in appearance and demeanor—but in physical attributes and perseverance. Fair-haired and barrel-chested, his gentle ways, charisma, and athletic grace attracted girls, made him popular with boys, yet shocked big and older schoolyard bullies, who suffered changed countenances and aches in private body parts when they messed with him.

In 1921, when Kenny was ten years old, his father was shot to death during a factory labor riot. He'd commanded a private security force. That winter, while Kenny rode a Chicago subway with his mother and sister, two mobsters shot and killed each other. A stray bullet found its way into his knee and forever crippled him. His mother was shot dead.

Kenny and Jane Palmer became orphans.

For two years both resided at *Chapin Hall Asylum For Children*. Separate adoptions placed Jane with the affluent Fisher family—owner of a Chicago-based hotel chain; and Kenny, with Bud and Paula Kroneldt in Dalton, Nebraska—following his journey there on an orphan train.

Immediate stirrings occurred on the second floor residence. Kenny and his sleepy-eyed, adoptive family members appeared at their bedroom doorways. Bud Kroneldt bounded down the stairs, followed by Kenny, who needed to grip the railing to accommodate his crippled leg. Bud opened the front door.

"Western Union," said the messenger. "Telegrams for Kenny Kroneldt from Hollywood and Chicago."

Kenny tore open the telegram from Hollywood.

DEAR KENNY - YOUR SISTER WAS INJURED FROM A FALL OFF HIGH PLATFORM WHILE FILMING "ANGEL IN THE MORNING" - JANE UNCONSCIOUS AT CEDARS OF LEBANON HOSPITAL - BROKEN BONES AND OTHER INJURIES - PLEASE COME - HER ADOPTIVE PARENTS IN CHICAGO ADRIAN AND HELEN FISHER INSIST ON MAKING TRAVEL ARRANGEMENTS AND

ACCOMPANYING YOU IF KRO-
NELDTS CONSENT - AWAIT THEIR
WIRE AFFIRMING DETAILS - CLIVE
& GLADYS ROGEL

"What is it, son?" asked Bud.

Kenny handed him the telegram, and opened the second. A silver-haired man, wearing a monocle, approached from the stairs. Aaron Zinkgraf was Kenny's adoptive grandfather, Paula Kroneldt's father, and the Mercantile's owner.

"Okay if I peek?" he asked.

Kenny nodded.

DEAR KENNY - JANE IS HOSPITAL-
IZED FOR INJURIES SUFFERED
FILMING - LETS VISIT HER TO-
GETHER - WE HAVE PULLMAN
RESERVATIONS ON TRAIN FROM
CHICAGO - ARRIVING IN DAL-
TON WEDNESDAY 3:30PM AND
LOS ANGELES FRIDAY PM - RE-
TURN WILL BE DETERMINED BY
HER CONDITION - ADRIAN AND
HELEN FISHER

*   *   *

The view outside the train window was an endless line of dry creek beds, abandoned farmhouses, and fields of dust—mile after mile of devastation caused by the five-year drought and Depression.

Kenny thought about Dalton acquaintances who'd moved away—farmers, classmates, extended families, young and old at Saturday night Grange dances, owners and employees of umpteen business establishments. Ironically, private ownership had kept the town's only bank afloat—along with its counterpart in Superior, seventeen miles away.

Kenny would be a college senior in September at the University of Nebraska in Lincoln, working simultaneously toward Bachelor and Master degrees. He'd reduced college expenses with merit scholarships and teaching assistantships in the mathematics and physics departments.

"God only knows how talent is derived," his faculty advisor told him during his sophomore year. "Your innovations in mathematics are brilliant and bold."

Kenny had anticipated several train coaches to be crowded with orphans, but there were none. Orphan trains stopped running in 1930.

The Fisher Hotels in Chicago, Detroit, and Cleveland could have gone broke during the Depression, but Adrian Fisher had foreseen the long-term, calamitous effects of the drought that turned the farm-belt into a virtual desert, and he refused to abide or collaborate with speculators, who'd exploited and abetted the overheated stock market that led to the bank bust. He sold several under-performing hotels to raise capital for cash reserves, and paid off remaining mortgages, while speculators bought stocks on margin and leveraged their holdings to acquire even more—burying themselves under bankrupting debt.

"Let's bring Jane something really nice, Kenny," said Helen Fisher. "What do you think she'd like?"

Her repeated attempts to keep Kenny from dwelling on Jane's accident weren't successful. Each station stop provided newspapers with scary banner headlines about her.

JANE CLOSE TO DEATH

AMERICA HOLDS ITS BREATH

Privacy was difficult. The conductor informed other passengers that "Jane Palmer's brother and parents" were on the train. A reporter sneaked aboard in Kansas City for an interview, but Kenny locked himself in the cramped washroom until the train departed the station.

Chapter Two

Kenny wished he could see through the curtained window into Jane's hospital room. Shadowy movements gave no hint what was occurring. He'd not yet been informed about her condition.

Ether permeated the air. Several nurses dashed in and out during the fifteen minutes he and the Fishers waited in the corridor. The foot of Jane's bed was all he glimpsed, whenever the door opened.

Flowers, teddy bears, and other gifts lined both sides of the corridor. Boxes of telegrams and letters were stacked on two gurneys beside her door.

The train had arrived at Union Station in Los Angeles two hours earlier. Clive and Gladys Rogel awaited in the film studio limousine, then rushed them to the hospital. Kenny and the Fishers pushed through a clamor of reporters and fans before being escorted up to the surgical floor.

"Can we see her now?" asked Kenny, as Dr. Roberts approached and introduced himself.

"Jane remains in a coma," he replied. "We've repaired broken bones, but she suffered a head injury."

"My sister will get well, won't she?" asked Kenny.

"She's getting good care. Be prepared for some visual discomfort."

They entered her room. Helen Fisher couldn't contain an audible gasp, then loud sobs. Her legs buckled. An attending nurse held her upright, then led her out. Adrian Fisher assisted.

Kenny stood transfixed. Jane was encased in several casts. Tubes protruded. Her long, brunette hair was braided... puffiness shrouded her eyelids... bruises covered her cheek and neck.

* * *

That Evening

Kenny gazed at Hollywood Boulevard from the ninth floor suite in the Roosevelt Hotel. It was late. He was alone in the dark, although Adrian and Helen Fisher were sleeping in one of the two bedrooms. Various sounds broke the silence—the traffic below, movement of the elevator, doors opening and closing, footsteps and chatter in the corridor.

Diagonally across the street, *Grauman's Chinese Theater* was emptying of late show patrons. *Charlie Chaplin* was featured on the marquee. In past years, Jane had shared top billing with him at Radio City Music Hall in New York.

Why would a gifted person like her be so seriously injured, Kenny wondered, and possibly nullify her bright future? She'd made something of her God-given gifts. She didn't waste them. She'd become a stunning, creative performer with mil-

lions of fans—even adored by her peers. Does God tantalize some by granting great gifts, only to jerk them away for no apparent reason? Why be blessed with gifts at all if that is one's destiny? Surely, it couldn't be Jane's. Kenny felt blind to God's purpose.

For almost an hour he stared down at the street. A worker carried a ladder from the theater courtyard, propped it against the marquee, and removed the letters. A well-dressed man strode from the theater, shouted something at the worker, and handed him a note. The worker inserted new letters, one-at-a-time.

G-E-T W-E-

A car pulled up to the front of the theater. The driver jumped out holding a large flash camera. The well-dressed, theater man strode toward him, spoke briefly, led him to a spot in the center of Hollywood Boulevard, and watched the worker finish his task.

G-E-T W-E-L-L J-A-N-E P-A-L-M-E-R

A-M-E-R-I-C-A P-R-A-Y-S

* * *

The following morning

Diners in the *Roosevelt Hotel's* crowded *Cinegrill* were engrossed with the *Los Angeles Times* front page story.

*NATION PRAYS FOR AMERICA'S
SWEETHEART*

The accompanying photograph was the one he'd witnessed a few hours earlier. Throughout the room, Kenny recognized several performers from films and posters he'd seen at theaters in Nebraska. Some peeked out the window at the marquee. Kenny and the Fishers awaited the Rogel's arrival for breakfast.

* * *

Fate had worked at long odds to introduce the Rogels to each other. Gladys Beecher was Jane's dormitory matron at Chapin Hall Orphanage. Clive Rogel was the Assistant General Manager and producer of Vaudeville shows and musicals at Chicago's Olympic Theater, where they'd met in 1921. Gladys escorted Jane to her first Lillian Lorraine concert there. Shortly after Clive married Gladys, in 1924, he was recruited to Hollywood to produce short features and musical sequences. Soon, he directed full-length films. His first three starred Jane Palmer.

She resided at the Rogel's Studio City home since her graduation from Chicago's Prairie Avenue Academy. Previously, she'd been their house guest while filming. Her pictures were always scheduled during school holidays and summertime.

The Fishers already had four children before they adopted Jane. She'd rescued Sheila Fisher from drowning at Lake Wandermere, where the Fishers owned a summer cottage. A vacation camp for orphans was directly across the lake. Sheila was a sophomore at the University of Colorado. Gretchen died in 1919 from a ruptured appendix during surgery. George, a West Point graduate and U.S. Army Captain, was stationed at Fort Meade, Maryland. Roman, a college dropout, was employed in ever-changing assignments at one of the Fisher Hotels.

*   *   *

Eight days of no change in Jane's condition created a routine for Kenny of hope and despair—pre-dawn views of Hollywood Boulevard from the ninth floor, *Cinegrill* breakfasts with the Rogels and Fishers, dire newspaper headlines, daily hospital visits, hordes of gawkers in the lobby, and Dr. Robert's briefings.

Helen Fisher confined herself to the hotel suite much of each day—napping and crying and writing postcards. Adrian Fisher attended various meetings somewhere. Kenny took long walks around Hollywood, and thumbed rides to the UCLA campus and back every day. A *Los Angeles Times* photographer took his picture for a front page story without his knowledge. Kenny's anonymity was gone.

Cinegrill diners showed respect for privacy, yet, Kenny got the impression that Clive Rogel knew everybody. Celebrities knew him by his first name. Pola Negri waved him over for a hug. Adolphe Menjou strolled from his table to meet the others. Irving Thalberg and Lillian Gish engaged Clive in a serious-looking conversation in the lobby. Buddy Ebsen performed a brief tap dance at their table.

"Jane Palmer is a survivor, or why would I look so happy dancing for you?" he said. *Tappity-tappity-tappity.*

*   *   *

Monday morning was different.

"You're in here!" shouted a male voice from the *Cinegrill* entryway.

Kenny turned to look at Darrell Cassidy, a college classmate, striding toward him — brushing aside the maitre'd. He was a large person, prematurely bald, with an infectious smile.

"I saw your picture and story in the paper, old buddy," he proclaimed. "I drove down from Santa Barbara. Dad loaned me the station wagon to cheer you up. I just checked in."

Kenny introduced him. "Darrell's my fraternity brother, halfback on the football team, and best friend since we were freshmen. He runs like a gazelle."

"Ha ha ha, listen to him," replied Darrell. "Kenny is stronger than me, wins all the science awards, and a whole lot smarter than his professors."

He carried a chair from another table and sat down.

"Are you and Kenny in physics and mathematics classes together?" asked Helen.

"Ha ha ha. You got to be a brain to do that. Physiques maybe, not phy-sics."

"Darrell's a history major," said Kenny. "He plans to teach and coach."

"Except for Kenny's bum leg," confided Darrell, "he'd play on the varsity, too."

"Gladys and I are hosting a get-together tonight, Darrell, for a few of Jane's friends at our home," said Clive. "Would you like to attend?"

*   *   *

Kenny wasn't planning to demonstrate his mathematics talent at the Rogel's party, but Darrell and Clive left him no choice.

"I love parties," said Buddy Ebsen. "They're escapes."

"Just like your dancing." Mary Pickford smiled at him.

"And your enchanting movies," replied the dancer.

"Let's play a game," said Wallace Beery.

"Good thought," agreed Jack Wagner, the studio boss.

"I've got one for you," said Clive, as he grabbed Darrell's arm, pulled him to the center of the courtyard, tapped his drinking glass to get everyone's attention, and announced, "Darrell Cassidy here is the best friend of Jane's brother. He told me about something Kenny can do that no one else in the world can do. I propose making a game of it."

"What is it?" shouted Harold Lloyd.

"I'm curious," said Douglas Fairbanks.

Clive pushed Darrell forward. "Explain it to everyone, Darrell."

All crowded closer. Kenny's facial expression was legitimate surprise.

"Everyone remembers memorizing the times tables in grade school, don't we?" asked Darrell. "Not only did Kenny master that feat the first day he was exposed to them, he helped the teacher teach his classmates. He dazzled them by multiplying two 2-digit numbers in his head, without writing them down. Does that sound impossible or what? But, listen to this."

Gladys Rogel sidled through the crowded courtyard as Darrell spoke. She handed each guest a pencil and pad.

"Kenny can multiply two *3-digit* numbers in his head faster than any of you, but you get to use pencil and paper. And he doesn't."

"Who wants to play?" asked Clive.

"If you can do that, Kenny," shouted Adolphe Menjou, "I'll donate fifty dollars for your college education. Make that one hundred dollars!"

"So will I," shouted Ruby Stevens.

"None of my accountants can do that," said Jack Wagner. "Have you been keeping Kenny a secret from me, Clive?"

"Listen, everybody," pleaded Clive Rogel. "You are my guests, this is a party, let's have fun with this. It's a game, not a lottery."

"My offer stands," replied Adolphe Menjou. "Who wouldn't want to be involved in some way with this young genius, Jane Palmer's older brother?"

"Can you do that, Kenny?" asked Douglas Fairbanks.

Clive intervened. "You know better than I do that a good tale doesn't give away the ending."

"You mean the butler *didn't* do it?" asked the actor.

Everyone laughed.

"I believe Kenny *can* do it," said Mary Pickford.

"We're anxious to see," said Tallulah Bankhead. "Can we agree that all of us are in for one-hundred dollars if Mary's right? We want Mary to be right, don't we?"

Cheers erupted.

"It's settled," she said. "This is more exciting than Doug's last picture."

"My next one will be titled, "The Swashbuckling Mathematician," replied the actor, as he assumed a swordsman's pose. "Swish-swish-swish."

"That's only subtraction," shouted Buddy Ebsen.

Hip-slapping revelry broke out.

"I'd go see that one," said Tallulah.

Clive held up his arms for quiet. "Are fraternity parties this raucous?"

Kenny and Darrell smiled in reply.

"Are you ready to play?" asked Clive.

Kenny shrugged. Clive turned to the guests.

"We need a volunteer to slowly announce any two 3-digit numbers you choose. That way, Kenny will hear them at the same moment as us. Write them down as they're presented. The numbers cannot be repeated. That would give Kenny extra time. Raise your hand when you finish."

"I volunteer," said Tallulah.

"Thank you. Everyone have a pad? Questions?"

A moment passed. None were asked.

"Go ahead, Tallulah."

"6-3-7 times 8-2-4," she intoned.

Mad scribbling began. Focused determination had gripped the party. Clive and Darrell eased away from Kenny, allowing him space to gaze at the starry sky. Two doves settled on the courtyard wall and stared at the assembly. Gladys awaited any signal of completion. Time passed slowly. Kenny broke the silence.

"5-2-4-8-8-8," he chanted.

All gaped at him. Gladys began to figure.

"I'm not even half done," muttered Wallace Beery.

"Me too," wailed Buddy Ebsen.

"Did he get it right?" asked Gloria Swanson.

"I just know he did," purred Mary Pickford.

"Give me a minute," said Gladys Rogel.

Quiet returned. All eyes were on Gladys. A minute passed. Then another.

"None of you signaled, before Kenny gave his answer," said Gladys. "5-2-4-8-8-8 is correct. Kenny got it right!"

Cheers broke out. Adolphe Menjou strode forward, waving his wallet overhead. He removed a hundred dollar bill with a flourish, and placed it on the empty tray beside Gladys.

Chapter Three

"I wish I could give you a prognosis," said Dr. Roberts. "We are maintaining a constant vigil, Jane's vital signs are stable, she remains in a coma, we've ruled out head surgery, we're moving her to the orthopedic ward."

Kenny and the Fishers faced him outside Jane's room.

"Maybe she won't...," began Helen Fisher in a quavering voice.

"Of course she will," interrupted Adrian. "Jane was in excellent condition before her accident," said the doctor.

"We'd hoped to take her to Chicago," said Adrian.

"Jane needs to remain here."

* * *

Kenny stood alone on the rear platform of the passenger train. An hour had passed since its morning departure from Union Station at a seemingly measured crawl past a hodgepodge of warehouses, tenements, shopping districts, schoolyards, graffiti, and weed-strewn vacant fields. The Los Angeles River—absent any trace of water—ran adjacent to the tracks for several miles before it veered South.

Migrant camps were barely visible through the dense chaparral. Queues of vehicles waited at street crossings. Drivers stood beside open doors. Neighborhoods varied. Children on bicycles, roller-skates, playing hopscotch, jacks, jump rope, and softball were everywhere. A pretty girl waved from her back yard. He waved back.

Kenny shared something in common with all of them— knowledge about his sister. If he shouted her name, the likeness of *Jane Palmer* would fill their brains—even the sound of her voice. Many knew the characters she'd portrayed, and the songs she'd sung. And details of her accident.

Her fame wasn't a substance one could see or touch, but instead, a spirit with elongated arms and fingers that reached out and embraced millions of fans.

Ideas, insight, and creation were equally mystifying.

Whenever he faced a tough physics or math problem, the solution did not exist a split second before the moment of inspiration. Then it did. Whap! Just like that. Whap! It simply popped into his head. *Nothing* became *something*— like a glint of sunlight smacking a warehouse window as the train rolled by.

The whole of existence must have had a creator—or how could it be? How could he?

When he was alone sometimes, he tried to imagine that only he existed. All else was simply an invention of his mind. The train was a great place to do that. As it headed East across the Mojave Desert, he pretended that everything beyond the Western horizon ceased to exist.

He couldn't keep his mind off of Jane, though.

* * *

Teddy Pawelsky had gotten her hair bobbed since Kenny had seen her last. She told him short hair was a requirement for hospital ward duty at Chicago's *Marcella Niehoff School of Nursing*.

The Fishers had informed Kenny they planned to remain in Nebraska for a few days, but hadn't mentioned arranging or knowing about Teddy's trip to Dalton.

"We thought you deserved a pleasant surprise," said Helen Fisher, after Kenny spotted Teddy pacing the station platform and peering into coach windows.

Teddy had visited Kenny in Dalton and Lincoln every year since 1929, but none of the letters she'd mailed to him in Los Angeles revealed her surprise visit.

She was the only child of Paddy and Kate Pawelsky from Pilsen, a Bohemian neighborhood on Chicago's lower West side. Before Kenny and Jane became orphans, they resided in the same apartment building as the Pawelsky's. Paddy drove a taxicab. Kate managed ticket sales for the Olympic Theater, a Vaudeville and musical venue in Chicago's Loop. In 1921, Kate introduced Jane to Lillian Lorraine, the Ziegfeld Follies star. Jane was in the third grade.

A statuesque brunette with hazel eyes, big bones, and lots of athleticism, Teddy's tomboy demeanor could have typecast her as Tarzan's wife. She'd enchanted Kenny since elementary school. They planned to wed after both graduated the following spring.

Kenny hopped off the train ahead of the conductor and rushed to Teddy for a prolonged embrace. Within minutes the two headed for a familiar destination on his 1928 Harley-Davidson motorcycle.

Hardy Creek ran parallel to the unpaved road for seven miles Northeast of Dalton's city limits, then emptied into the Little Blue River at the wooden bridge. A vertical post underneath had clear markings that indicated the river's depth. It served as a gauge for estimating the annual crop yield for the area. Normal depth in mid-summer was nine feet, three inches, but it hadn't exceeded five feet since 1927.

"Let's go look," shouted Teddy, as she clambered off the idling motorcycle beside the wooden bridge and slid down the steep embankment.

*   *   *

Four year old Ernie Kroneldt shared ice cream with Adrian Fisher at the soda fountain in Zinkgraf's Mercantile.

"Is chocolate your favorite?" he asked.

"Strawberry and vanilla, too," he replied.

Ernie's mother was the Fishers' unmarried daughter, Sheila. She gave him up for adoption at birth, and avoided learning the identity of his adoptive parents; yet, her own parents facilitated the event. The Kroneldts encouraged their frequent visits.

The New Superior Hotel, seventeen miles away in Superior, provided Teddy and the Fishers with the only acceptable accommodations. The spare bedroom above the Mercantile belonged to Aaron Zinkgraf. Kenny slept in the upper bunk in Ernie's room. Dalton hotels contained only unplumbed bathtubs. Bud Kroneldt's parents offered two bedrooms at their nearby farmhouse, but Helen Fisher knew, from a previous visit, that the outhouse was the toilet.

* * *

The following afternoon Adrian Fisher accepted Kenny's invitation for his first motorcycle ride. He borrowed overalls and boots.

"Where we headed?" he shouted, when they were three miles out of town.

"This road doesn't end, but the Depression will, one of these days," replied Kenny.

"That spirit's contagious."

"The river's running at five feet, six inches."

"Is that good?"

"It's been rising."

"That's farmer talk."

"That's what people around here do. Water is gold."

"Will those who left return?"

"Grandpa said the bank won't foreclose on some who said they wanted to."

The mid-afternoon sun was behind them. Their silhouettes raced alongside as Kenny maneuvered around ruts and potholes. Varmints darted across the road ahead of them and vanished in the yellow grass. "What do you think about when you ride?" asked Adrian.

"The whole world in front of me."

"What are you going to do next with it?"

"Dalton needs the bank. It's surviving. Grandpa knows why. I'm planning to open a savings account for me and Teddy. Show confidence, let everyone know. It may cause others to do the same. That's what I want to talk to you about."

Kenny had twenty-seven hundred dollars stashed away. He'd won it at the Hollywood party. No one knew except the Fishers and Aaron Zinkgraf. Not even Teddy.

"Let's visit the bank tomorrow?" said Adrian.

"Grandpa will like that."

The wooden bridge over the Little Blue came into view. Kenny geared down and stopped beside the railing.

"It may be my imagination," said Kenny, staring at the river below, "but the water level is higher than yesterday."

"How can you tell?"

"Let's go look."

*   *   *

"The building appears to be well maintained," said Adrian Fisher, as he strode toward the bank with Aaron Zinkgraf and Kenny.

"It's an illusion," replied Aaron. "Business is practically zilch. Local investors own this bank and the one in Superior, the whole kit and kaboodle. Directors share the work load to keep overhead down. I own a small stake."

"Boarded up banks dot the country," said Adrian Fisher.

"State examiners are stunned at the clean balance sheet. If the Depression ends in the next couple of years, Board members have the resources and mettle to ride it out. We keep our fingers crossed anyway."

Dalton State Bank occupied a two-story brick building two blocks from Zinkgraf's Mercantile. A sign in the window read:

Serving Southern Nebraska and North-
ern Kansas since 1891, and expect we'll be

*here a whole lot longer. That's a fact—not
a promise.*

Howard Proctor, President

Inside was pristine—polished brass, silk curtains, leather chairs, schoolchildren art on one wall, mahogany desks, polished-steel vault. Two ceiling fans rotated slowly.

"Good morning, all." A cheerful female voice came from behind the third teller window. A silver-haired, elegant lady appeared to be the only employee in the building. "It's a lovely day for a bank transaction, isn't it." She pressed her face against the vertical bars.

"Good morning, Hazel," replied Aaron. "My grandson has a pocketful of cash, and Adrian Fisher here from Chicago wants to meet your husband. Is Howard around?"

"When isn't he?"

An office door opened behind her. Howard Proctor appeared, donning his suit coat. He was short, bespectacled, pale-complexioned, with a military bearing.

"Do I hear the rustle of money, Aaron?" he asked, as he strode toward them. "Kenny, my boy, we're all praying for your sister... you got a sterling record at the University, I hear... of course I know who *you* are, Mr. Adrian Fisher, the hotel magnate from Chicago... it is a pleasure to meet you in person, sir... I hope we can find a way to do some business... meet my lifelong sweetheart since kindergarten, Hazel... Honey, will you bring in an extra chair?"

Kenny never met anyone who could say so much without taking a breath.

Howard Proctor shook hands all around, and waved them into his office. His wife dragged in a chair, then exited.

Kenny expected the first topic to be his deposit, but it wasn't. For thirty minutes, Adrian Fisher engaged Howard Proctor in banker talk, delinquent farm loans, composition of the Board of Directors, the economy, and high-finance generalities.

"Hazel, bring in the Corporate Records for the last four years," he shouted, "along with the Loan Journal and Current Payments Ledger… stock records, too… I'm coming to help." He strode out.

"I believe I'll be staying a few extra days, Kenny," said Adrian Fisher. "Helen can accompany Teddy back to Chicago next Monday as planned."

"Should I make my deposit?" asked Kenny.

"Let's get a photograph of you and Teddy handing it over to the Proctors. I'm putting my chief accountant and a property appraiser from Chicago on the train in the morning."

Chapter Four

Kenny's photograph stared back at him from the front pages of the *Chicago Tribune* and the *Omaha World-Herald*.

The University of Nebraska library was practically empty in the early evening. The semester wouldn't start for a week. He needed to finalize his teaching plans for two calculus classes, and meet with his Masters program advisor, Dr. Mordecai Hellman, who was Dean of the mathematics department.

The photos in both newspapers showed *"Jane Palmer's brother"* opening a savings account in Dalton, Nebraska. A second photo featured, *"Chicago hotel entrepreneur and Jane Palmer's father"*, Adrian Fisher, with the Dalton and Superior banks' Board of Directors. The accompanying story mentioned his substantial stock purchase.

Kenny knew the key attraction was the dearth of foreclosures by the two banks since 1929. Certainly, many farm loans were delinquent and had defaulted, farm families and workers had moved on—along with several of Kenny's high school classmates—but instead of the automatic, legal bank foreclosure for nonpayment, well-heeled bank directors of the Dalton and Superior Banks had first determined the intent of the qualified debtors. Did they plan to pay a negotiated sum later when conditions improved—or simply desert the property without notification. The latter were foreclosed on.

The former got a reprieve from angels—the small group of directors who kept the loans current with their own resources—although that practice had already begun stretching some to their financial limits, until Adrian Fisher appeared on the scene.

For big city newspapers to feature a small-town America event astonished Kenny, although their motive was the same as his own. He'd hoped news about his own modest deposit would stir some confidence in the bank. His aim was Nebraska and Kansas, not a national audience.

"What can the banks do with the foreclosed farms without good operators?" asked Adrian Fisher. "Nothing, of course. Experienced farmers are facing circumstances beyond their control. Why not strive to nurture and save them? This Depression can't last forever. When it's over, who are most qualified and motivated to operate the farms? Those who've farmed them for generations, that's who."

Kenny smiled at Adrian Fisher's little grin in the photo. Same one he had when Kenny asked what his risk was to invest in the banks.

"Ha ha ha … the water level is rising," replied Fisher. "You showed me, yourself."

* * *

Hollywood, California

The rope felt tight in her hand, just as the director said it should.

"No slack, ever," he'd admonished.

Peering downward from the platform made it seem much higher than it had appeared when she'd looked up at it from the stage. Two trainers had accustomed her gradually to the height, having raised it several feet at a time during the rehearsal.

The decking of her platform consisted of narrow slats, separated by half-inch gaps. A waist-high, metal railing with vertical bars, spaced three inches apart, surrounded her on three sides.

Clive and Gladys Rogel had begged her to allow a stand-in to perform the stunt, but she'd convinced the Director that she was physically capable, and persuaded him not to inform them until after the scene was shot. She was the star, after all, and knew she could accomplish it without difficulty. Besides, it was a new challenge. She'd pointed out that her stand-in was almost twice her age. *The audience would surely notice the difference.*

Beneath her costume, she felt the tight fitting body harness, to which was attached wires that ran up and over iron swivels attached to a large, wooden beam near the studio's high arching ceiling, then down to giant spools operated with hand cranks by stagehands at various locations behind the principal camera position.

Her slightest wiggle caused the wires to make tiny whizzing sounds as they stretched out any slack. An assistant director had informed her that her angel wings would hide the wires from view as she appeared to fly like an angel across the sound stage. Part of the artistry, he'd told her, was to not sway. She'd already completed her close-ups during which the scenery moved— not her.

That had been easy. What wasn't easy was waiting - waiting - waiting for the filming to commence. She hadn't practiced that. And it was so hot in the suffocating harness. Nobody had informed her about the itching it caused. Or how to deal with it. Loosening four laces at the front of the device seemed necessary. It made breathing easier and enabled her to lean from side to side to exercise some stiffness away— even bend over the railing to look straight down. She knew she'd only need a moment to tighten and retie the laces whenever the Director announced in his authoritative voice that he was finally ready.

"Another moment, Jane, okay?" he hollered through his megaphone for what seemed like the umpteenth time.

"Yes, Paul," she hollered back, but instead of remaining immobile and cheerless, as she'd been previously, she released her grip on the rope, leaned over the railing as she replied with a radiant smile, heard an horrific tearing sound of cloth, felt herself falling away from the bulky costume and harness, and saw the stage floor fast approaching her gorgeous, angelic face.

*

"Her eyes opened, Dr. Roberts," said the nurse. Her hands gripped Jane's. "She whispered two words repeatedly while you sawed off her cast."

"Hallelujah," replied the doctor. "Jane is awakening from her coma."

"Yes, Paul," whispered Jane.

Dr. Roberts leant over the bed and put his face close to hers. "I'm not Paul, Jane. I'm Dr. Roberts. Do you know where you are?"

Jane gazed past his face at the brightly lit room.

"You are at Cedars of Lebanon hospital," said the doctor.

"I can't be at the hospital?" she asked with a barely perceptible voice. "I'm in the middle of a scene."

"You suffered a serious fall from a raised platform."

"Does Paul know?"

"He's waiting to hear you're all right."

"What happened to my costume?"

"You suffered multiple injuries in the accident, Jane. I just removed your body cast."

* * *

"*Jane Revives*," read the banner headline in the *Los Angeles Times*. Radio listeners learned sooner. A crush of fans and reporters filled the hospital lobby and grounds out front. Police barricaded the street, allowing only emergency vehicles through. Dr. Roberts had immediately phoned Clive and Gladys Rogel, who hurriedly notified others and rushed to the hospital.

*

TELEGRAM FROM GLADYS AND CLIVE ROGEL TO KENNY KRONELDT, AUGUST 28, 1932, 9:16 a.m. PST.

DEAR KENNY - YOUR SISTER IS
AWAKE - HER CAST IS OFF - CLIVE
AND I EN ROUTE TO HOSPITAL -

MORE LATER - WE ARE WIRING
THE FISHERS NOW - GLADYS AND
CLIVE ROGEL

*

TELEGRAM FROM GLADYS AND CLIVE ROGEL TO
ADRIAN AND HELEN FISHER, AUGUST 28, 1932, 9:21
A.M. PST.

JANE REVIVED THIS MORNING -
CLIVE AND I WILL BE HER FIRST
VISITORS - CAN YOU COME? -
PLAN TO BE OUR HOUSE GUESTS
- GLADYS AND CLIVE ROGEL

*

TELEGRAM FROM ADRIAN AND HELEN FISHER TO
KENNY KRONELDT, AUGUST 28, 1932, 11:05 A.M. CST.

KENNY - WE HEARD MARVELOUS
NEWS ABOUT JANE FROM THE
ROGELS - GLADYS WIRED THAT
SHE INFORMED YOU - I SPOKE
TO DOCTOR BY LONG DISTANCE
PHONE - MRS FISHER WILL DE-
PART FOR LOS ANGELES BY TRAIN
TOMORROW - WE HOPE YOU RE-
MAIN AT SCHOOL - WILL KEEP
YOU INFORMED - OUR PLAN IS

TO BRING HER HOME TO CHI-
CAGO TO RECOVER - YOU CAN
SEE HER THANKSGIVING AND
CHRISTMAS - OUR PRAYERS HAVE
BEEN ANSWERED - ADRIAN AND
HELEN FISHER

*

TELEGRAM FROM ADRIAN AND HELEN FISHER TO
BUD AND PAULA KRONELDT, 11:20 A.M. CST.

DEAR BUD AND PAULA - JANE IS
AWAKE - CAST IS OFF - HELEN
WILL BE IN LOS ANGELES IN 3
DAYS - WE NOTIFIED KENNY - WE
HOPE HE DOES NOT MAKE THE
TRIP AND DELAY HIS STUDIES -
ADRIAN AND HELEN FISHER

* * *

The din from the hospital corridor awakened her constantly.

*But, why should she sleep? Dr. Roberts in-
formed her she'd been in a coma since July
10— seven weeks! She couldn't recall any
dreams. Maybe she hadn't had any. Her
waking moments brought excruciating
headaches and dizziness that only sleep re-
lieved. The last thing she remembered before her long sleep was loosening the harness*

laces and leaning over the platform— then gazing up at a nurse, who became a doctor. A door opened and closed numerous times. White-clad figures pulled the curtains apart, opened the window, poked and prodded her while she stared out into the sunshine. She felt dampness and tugging on her hair and face. Four doctors held charts and talked mysteriously. They vanished when Dr. Roberts appeared with an orderly toting a food tray.

"Clive and Gladys Rogel just went down to the cafeteria," he whispered to Jane. "Mrs. Rogel washed and combed your hair and made you up. You resemble a princess, Jane, as you always do in your motion pictures. Look." He held a mirror close to her face. "Mr. Wagner, from your studio, and Klaus Leonhardt are waiting downstairs for your permission to visit."

Although Jack Wagner was the much-publicized studio boss of Hollywood's most prolific film company, all eyes were on his male guest, as the two followed the escort from the elevator, and strode to Jane's fifth floor room. Nurses stopped and gaped. Ambulatory patients made way. Dr. Roberts met the pair at the door, then led them inside.

Suddenly Jane was wide awake and strived to sit up in bed. She'd never met the handsome actor.

Klaus Leonhardt starred in several popular foreign films the past two years, and was the subject of countless newspaper and magazine articles. The thirty-one year blond Adonis was six foot two, with leading man charisma. Every American studio pursued him.

Although his family roots were multigenerational German, his maternal grandmother was Jewish. Grandfather Leonhardt founded LMW, Ltd. (Leonhardt Machine Werks), a principal supplier of engine casings and fittings to European automobile and tractor manufacturers. The company was located in Schrobenhausen, near Munich.

The actor's father was bitterly disappointed that Klaus had dropped out of college as a third year mechanical engineering student at Munich University of Technology— *Technische Universitat Munchen*— to become a Shakespearean actor in Berlin Theater.

His reputation of impeccable manners and charm preceded him to America. Women screamed and misbehaved at his public appearances. Men admired his masculinity and devil-may-care demeanor.

Klaus leant down and kissed Jane's hand. "You are America's sweetheart," he said. "And the world's."

"Audiences will pack theaters to watch the two of you together, Jane," said Jack Wagner.

"Mr. Wagner has signed me for three starring roles," said Klaus, still holding her hand. "Will you be my leading lady?"

"Maid Marian to his Robin Hood," said Wagner.

"No other actress will do," said Klaus.

"An army nurse to his lieutenant," said Wagner.

"No other actress will do," said Klaus.

"An Irish lass to his Catholic priest."

"No other actress will do."

"Will I get well?" asked Jane.

"I've left the production dates open." said Wagner.

Chapter Five

OCTOBER 1932
CHICAGO

Jane leaned over the wooden railing on the twelfth floor landing in the narrow, emergency stairwell of the Fisher Hotel, and stared at the tiny patch of basement floor. She was considering a third round-trip for the first time.

What had begun as part of a daily exercise regimen, three weeks earlier, of deliberate steps up and down one flight of stairs had progressed to thirteen flights of stairs, from the top floor to the basement, with leg stretching and shadow boxing at each landing.

Few outside her family circle and selected hotel staffers were privy to her activity. The public only knew she was at the hotel, monitored twenty-four hours a day by a medical team.

"Please let me go again," she told the nurse.

They headed down the stairs together. At the seventh floor landing the hotel manager opened the door.

"Miss Palmer," he whispered, "Lillian Lorraine is waiting upstairs with your mother and father."

*   *   *

Jane smiled as the star of the Ziegfield Follies star embraced her.

"My precious darling," crooned the French beauty, "you've been through such an ordeal. Let me look at you… just what I hoped… exquisite perfection… you look radiant … ready to perform."

"What's the best news you'd like to hear today?" asked Helen Fisher.

"I'm ready?" replied Jane.

"As long as it's not physical," said Adrian Fisher.

"Your fans await your lovely voice," said Lillian.

"The doctor has approved," said Helen. "The Follies are booked at the Olympic Theater next week. We're making arrangements for Kenny to be there."

*   *   *

Kenny gazed around the magnificent theater from his front row seat. Beside him were Teddy, her parents, and the Fishers. It was a full house.

The Ziegfield Follies usually performed in larger venues, such as New York City's Radio City Music Hall and Chicago's Orchestra Hall, but Lillian Lorraine had persuaded Sid Ziegfield, her longtime consort, to book the Olympic to showcase Jane's first public appearance since her accident. It's where she'd first met Jane. They'd performed together dozens of times during Jane's rise to stardom.

Kenny had hoped for details of his sister's performance in advance, but was unsuccessful.

"I promised Lillian I wouldn't tell *anyone*," she insisted at the dinner table the previous evening. "*Everyone* always needs to keep their promises, don't they?"

"All we know is she won't be high-stepping with the chorus line," said Adrian Fisher.

"Why don't we just wait," said Helen, "and discover her performance together with the rest of the audience?"

The first half of the extravagant production was non-stop pizzazz: rows of stem-legged beauties in flawless synchronization; snappy ensembles of tuxedo-clad tap dancers, interrupted by sassy patter between Eddy Cantor, Jimmy Durante, and Lillian Lorraine; plus fast-changing backdrops, accompanied by flumes of smoke and colorful lighting; yet, no sign of Jane.

Following intermission, the curtain opened on a young man seated on a sofa holding on his lap a wide-eyed puppet, decked out in a tuxedo, cloak, and top hat. Even a monocle.

Applause began as the announcer introduced the pair as, "Chicago's very own ventriloquist... Edgar Bergen... and everybody's good friend...Charlie McCarthy."

"Charlie, do you know all these people?" asked Edgar Bergen.

"Why else would they be clapping?" asked Charlie.

"I thought we were partners, Charlie. Don't *I* have something to do with it?"

"You?... Well... " Charlie looked slowly around the audience, then at Edgar.

"Well what?" asked Edgar.

"I dressed up for the occasion, but look at you."

"Is that all you can say?

"What kind of dummy do you take me for?"

"Let me ask you this, Charlie. Did you know that the Zieg-field Follies featured so many big names?"

"You mean like Schlenzi Krazzenchavitchalkowsky?"

"No, Charlie."

"Rumplestiltskin?"

"No, Charlie."

"No?? Those names have lots of letters. They're big."

"Those are *long* names, Charlie. By big names I mean stars like Jimmy Durante ... Lillian Lorraine... Eddie Cantor..."

"Go on."

"Oh! Look. Here comes W.C. Fields."

The vaudevillian tipped his hat as he shuffled across the stage to much applause.

"Well, Charlie McCarthy," he said in his high-pitched, exaggeratedly singsong voice, "the woodpecker's pinup boy!"

"Well, if it isn't W.C. Fields, the man who keeps Seagram's in business!" snapped Charlie McCarthy.

"I love children. I can remember when ... with my own little unsteady legs ... I toddled from room to room."

"When was that? Last night?"

"Quiet, Wormwood, or I'll whittle you into a Venetian blind."

"Ooh, that makes me shutter!"

"Tell me Charles, is it true that your father was a dining room table leg?"

"If it is, your father was under it."

"Why, you stunted spruce, I'll throw a pair of tree-boring beetles on you."

"Why, you bar-fly you, I'll stick a wick in your mouth, and use you for an alcohol lamp!"

"Step out of the hot lights, Charles. You may come unglued."

"Mind if I stand in the shade of your nose?"

"Trees like you cast shadows, shadows, only shadows."

"I know how to sing."

"Ahhh, the sounds of twiggy branches snapping off."

"I sing as good as Jane Palmer can sing. As a matter of fact, I sound just like her."

W.C. Fields roared with disbelief.

"Wait a minute, Charlie," said Edgar Bergen. "We don't do impressions. We don't sing. Besides, Jane is a soprano."

"Do you want to hear me sing or not?" asked Charlie.

"But, Charlie, we haven't practiced. We haven't rehearsed. We've never even tried to sing before."

"You sleep *sometimes*. I've been practicing on the sly."

"I'm leaving before I get an earache," said W.C. Fields as he strolled off stage. "If that glorified apple box can sing, I'll eat my hat."

"Charlie, please don't do it," pleaded Edgar Bergen.

"Sshhh, I'm trying to concentrate," replied Charlie. "Music, maestro."

The orchestra played the prelude to Irving Berlin's, *A Pretty Girl is Like a Melody.*

"Charlie, please don't." He turned to the audience. "What can I do? Charlie's taking over. This has never happened before."

The puppet cleared his throat noisily, hummed several notes— sounding like himself, and as the orchestra segued into the lyric score, Charlie McCarthy's voice became Jane Palmer's. The astonished audience became wide-eyed, looking at each other, at Charlie, all around the stage and theater searching for Jane. Kenny and Teddy held onto each other. But, still on Edgar Bergen's lap, Charlie McCarthy sang lustily —sounding exactly like Jane Palmer.

As the second verse began, his cloak cascaded to the floor, his painted face tumbled like a mask, and Jane Palmer appeared in his place—on Edgar Bergen's lap. In full voice. The audience gasped as one.

Jane stood up, gripped the microphone and sang her heart out.

Kenny could hardly breath. Edgar Bergen arose from his chair and faced her, the entire Ziegfield Follies cast and guest stars slowly filed onto the stage, formed into rows, and as Jane finished her song, Lillian Lorraine approached her with a bouquet of roses.

Wild cheers and applause exploded from the bedazzled audience. Thrown flowers strewed the stage. Bravos went on for almost ten minutes. Teddy Pawelsky and Helen Fisher and many throughout the theater, including staffers and cast members, had tears streaming down their faces.

* * *

The following afternoon Jane spoke to students and teachers in the auditorium at Teddy's nursing school. Paddy Pawelsky drove her and Kenny there in his taxicab. Kate Pawelsky and Helen Fisher arrived in the hotel limousine.

"Teddy Pawelsky is my best friend," said Jane. "In grade school she protected me and all the girls from lecherous boys—branding them with black eyes, body bruises, you name it. They cried. Poor babies.

"Teddy is going to marry my brother, Kenny, in June when they both graduate. We'll be sisters for real. That makes me so very happy.

"When I fell off that high platform at the studio, I know that if Teddy had been close by, she would have caught me. Teddy was here. I want to thank you for your letters and telegrams and your prayers during my recovery. Here I am. Good as new.

"And here *you* are. Your dedication to your education here at the *Marcella Niehoff School of Nursing* defines you as someone very special. You share a gift with each other, a great gift, a wonderful gift—that of caring for the sick, infirm, and the injured.

"What Florence Nightingale began during the Crimean War almost eighty years ago, you will carry on through your own selves, and your classmates.

"Army nurses, utilizing her teachings in 1918, saved the life of my father, Lieutenant Ernest Palmer, on the battlefield. His injuries were unfathomable. Bullets and shrapnel tore into his body and face. His recovery required two years of nursing and doctoring, multiple surgeries and treatments in a London Army hospital. The day he came home from the war was the happiest day of my life.

"Each of us has been born with a God-given gift. I wish to express my gratitude to you for yours. I could have died last July in the studio accident. I owe my life to the nurses and doctors who nurtured me and hovered close by, ready to treat my every need. Thank you for your gift, and for each and every one of you."

Chapter Six

TWO WEEKS LATER

The head-waiter strode toward Jane's booth at the rear of the Fisher Hotel dining room, where she ate alone. Early morning breakfast was her preference before it crowded up.

"A Mr. Stanley Monson wishes to speak with you, Miss Palmer," he whispered. "He spotted you and started over, but I stopped him. He told me he has a timely message about Mr. Wagner and your unfinished film at his studio. Mr. Monson is a lawyer. Here's his card."

Jane looked toward the entry at a fat, bald man wearing a tailored suit, bow-tie, spats, and wire-framed spectacles. He held a fedora, cane, and briefcase.

"Tell him, Henry, that Mr. Wagner communicates with me several times a week, and, 'No thank you.'"

The head-waiter retreated. He returned after a few moments.

"Miss Palmer? Sorry to burden you. The man said he has new information *today* about your accident that Mr. Wagner could not have already revealed. Shall I send him away?"

Jane remained expressionless, but took a deep breath. "Tell the man that I have an appointment very shortly, but I will spare him *two* minutes. Just two. Thank you for intervening, Henry."

He returned to the fat man, who smiled and walked jauntily to Jane's booth, and sat down.

"Stanley Monson, attorney-at-law," he pronounced. "So nice to meet you, Miss Palmer. Yours is such a great talent, and such a sad story. I'll be brief." He set his briefcase beside him on the seat, and placed his fedora atop it, then laid his cane upon the table. "My law firm is headquartered here in Chicago. We specialize in litigation. My record for victories and large cash rewards is well-known in the legal community. Based on what I know about your accident, Jack Wagner's studio is liable, and..."

"Mr. Monson, stop!" said Jane. "What if my accident wasn't the studio's fault?"

"How could it not be? You stand to gain a fortune, my dear, perhaps even more, for your pain and suffering and lost income... not to mention an additional sum for ongoing and unknown future medical expenses. The case won't see the light of day in court. My own experience tells me the studio will settle."

"Mr. Monson. Stop! What if it *was my fault?*"

"Ha ha ha. No one would believe it."

"It *was* my own fault, Mr. Monson."

"Even so, no one will believe it."

Jane looked him in the eye, as she tore his business card into several pieces, and let them drop onto the table. "Your two minutes are up, Mr. Monson."

* * *

Lincoln, Nebraska

Kenny was stunned by the comments from Professor Mordecai Hellman.

"You've exceeded what we can teach you, within the limits of our mathematics curriculum, Kenny," he said.

The professor stood up and selected a thick volume from the bookshelf in cramped office.

"Ahhh, Archimedes," he said, "one who advanced the science of mathematics, taking abstract thought, exacting a discipline, and turning it into practical applications. Where would we be without him?… and Pythagoras?"

He replaced the book and sat down.

"Your Masters thesis supports my belief that you underestimate yourself, Kenny. If you expand your sampling considerably, I'm recommending it for your PhD doctoral thesis. The math department will provide you with the wherewithal to accomplish that.

"I'm engaged to be married in June and…" said Kenny.

"So I've heard," replied the professor. "Your innovations and inventive theorems provide breakthroughs in pure mathematics, and provide a foundation for examining new approaches for solving exquisitely complex problems, consisting of random numbers. Your work could lead to puzzle applications… and alterations on, heretofore, unassailable assumptions. The military, for example, might be able to encipher and decipher coded messages, *and* communicate with each other, similarly. Archimedes reborn."

The University president, Dr. Budd Auerbach, peeked in. "Did you break the news, Mo?" he asked.

"Just getting to it," replied Hellman.

"May I sit in?"

The professor nodded toward an empty chair. Dr. Auerbach shook hands with Kenny, and sat down.

"You're the talk of the Board of Regents," he said. "We wish to offer you a teaching position, at a full-time starting salary, commencing in September. You'll be assigned to four undergraduate courses. We believe you'll complete the work on your PhD in one year. You would agree to a three year teaching contract. And your future bride will be offered a nursing position at the campus clinic, or if she prefers... Lincoln General hospital."

* * *

December 9, 1932

Dear Jane;

We miss you! Hopefully not for much longer. Your fans are clamoring to watch you perform with Charlie McCarthy and the ventriliquist. Agog may not be an overstatement. I am enclosing newspaper clippings.

Edgar Bergen has agreed to one week at the Pantages Theater in Hollywood commencing February 15. I've booked you, subject to your recovery.

Gladys receives reassuring letters from Helen Fisher about your progress. We enjoyed dinner Saturday night with Jack Wagner and Klaus Leonhardt at the *Brown Derby*. Great insights about the studio's future and your role in it.

Klaus departed Sunday for Germany to visit his parents for the holidays. He seems reluctant to talk about them, but he mentioned that his father's factory is functioning at capacity, despite the poor economy. Government contracts— mostly military. We all laughed that the war ended in 1918, thank heavens.

Klaus sounds eager to start a picture with you. Just as Gladys and I are looking forward to your glowing, cheery presence in our home soon.

Warmest regards,

Clive Rogel
18204 Chaparral Lane
Studio City, California

*

December 10, 1932

Jane Palmer
Fisher Hotel
Chicago, Illinois

My dear Jane;

Let me know before Christmas which of the three films you choose to do first. I need to plan my production schedule. I'm aiming at mid-April to begin filming. Klaus is planning accordingly.

The unfinished *Angels in the Morning* requires but two days of your time for completion. I've scheduled the release date, June 1, for wide distribution. Pent-up demand is enormous.

A plethora of publicity has accrued from your Chicago show-stopper. What a trooper you are! The Pantages run will reap even greater rewards for you and the studio.

Affectionately,

Jack Wagner
Wagner Pictures
Hollywood, California

*

December 16, 1932

Jack,

I love all three scripts. My first choice is *The Soldier's Nurse*. The role for Klaus as the army lieutenant that my character, Anna, befriends on his sickbed after saving his life on the battlefield is so romantic and poignant. I cried when I read it.

I'm getting stronger with each passing day. Being on stage again with Lillian Lorraine was good therapy.

Love and kisses to everyone,

Jane Palmer

*　*　*

Helen Fisher cried most days during the Christmas season. Roman Fisher wrote an angry letter about his "unfair and disrespectful treatment," adding that he'd "prefer to drink eggnogs and boiler-makers in my girlfriend's apartment." He returned prepaid train tickets. During a long-distance phone call, he shouted, "Jane gets all your attention… she was *born* with her singing voice and had to do nothing to get it… she was adopted… she's just an orphan!"

"You've told us time and again," replied Adrian Fisher, "that people gossip about you being born with a silver spoon in your mouth. We can't stop it, Roman. You've told us you will '*show them*' what you're capable of. Your mother and I have always believed you."

Sheila Fisher drove to Idaho from Colorado with her college boyfriend to spend Christmas with his family.

George Fisher came home on leave from Fort Meade, Maryland, and reported he was on the promotion list for the rank of Major, and being reassigned to the U.S. Embassy in London as the military attaché's aide.

Chapter Seven

MAY 1933

Jane couldn't avoid overhearing the quiet conversation between Adrian Fisher and Nathan Ehrenfeld, an Omaha bank president. She and Helen Fisher sat beside them, awaiting the outdoor, graduation ceremony on the University campus in Lincoln. Kenny would receive his Bachelors and Masters degrees in mathematics and physics.

"Your publicity for Dalton State Bank," said Ehrenfeld, "has been attracting deposits from all over the country."

"Jane's brother put me on to it," replied Adrian. "Kenny risked his entire net worth... I risked less than one percent."

"It's working," replied Ehrenfeld.

"Those bank directors know how to nurture assets."

"Ha ha ha. Even those that have lost their value?"

"Homes and farms are invaluable to the owners."

"Defaults must be dealt with responsibly."

"Franklin Roosevelt's doing the opposite of Herbert Hoover... lowering taxes, creating the Federal Reserve, SEC, New Deal. He's trying all sorts of things."

"Lots of skepticism out there."

"Roosevelt has a Congress that will work with him, Hoover didn't. He's planted the seeds. Confidence will grow, you'll see."

"I wish I shared your optimism."

*   *   *

The previous day, Kenny accompanied Teddy to the Campus Clinic and Lincoln General Hospital. True to the word of Professor Hellman, both facilities offered her a position. Teddy chose the hospital. It provided her the opportunity to intern as a surgical nurse.

*   *   *

June

Kenny awaited Teddy beside the altar at St. Procopius Church in Pilsen. Beside him stood Darrell Cassidy, his best man. Jane was the bride's maid of honor. Teddy Pawelsky approached, arm-in-arm with her father.

Life-altering events alternated between purposeful and accidental, thought Kenny.

His father, Ernest Palmer, who'd returned from the Great War, maimed and facially disfigured, couldn't get rehired at his former job. He became a security guard. His boss arranged for the apartment in Pilsen. Kenny would have not met Teddy without those series of events.

Teddy's mother worked at the Olympic Theater, where Jane met Lillian Lorraine. She may not have become a film star without her guidance, another accidental event.

Gladys met Clive Rogel there. She'd chaperoned Jane for the Lillian Lorraine concert. That accidental event changed her life. She wouldn't have known Jane or met her husband if she'd not been employed at Chapin Hall Orphanage. Jane and Kenny wouldn't have lived there if their parents had not been murdered.

If Kenny hadn't been adopted by the Kroneldts, he would not have attended the University of Nebraska, or met Darrell Cassidy, or been on the accelerated schedule for his PhD degree, or any of the other twists and turns that brought him to this present place.

Now, Teddy was within a few steps of standing beside him to publicly affirm their wedded lifetime together, a future to be filled with accidental events and purposeful choices.

*   *   *

During filming of *The Soldier's Nurse*, Jane and Klaus were inseparable. Publicity photos appeared every week—dining in Hollywood and Beverly Hills restaurants, frolicking in the Santa Monica surf, strolling through Griffith Park Observatory.

It had all been dreamt up by Jack Wagner, commencing with the co-stars' appearance together at the Hollywood premiere of *Angels in the Morning*. Jane and Klaus knew there was more to their relationship than that.

In public, Klaus Leonhardt was flirtatious, swaggering, and spoke double entendres. With Jane, he was shy, self-deprecating, and reluctant to speak about himself. Initially, she strived to resist his charms—but couldn't.

He accepted weekly invitations from the Rogels for Sunday dinner. Evenings usually found them alone together, motoring through the Hollywood hills in his cream-colored Bugatti, and parking on a bluff overlooking the city lights. Sometimes they practiced their lines for the following day's filming.

.

Chapter Eight

The quietude in the faculty lounge was interrupted by an angry outburst. Kenny was seated at a table with six others. Professor Benjamin Cohen stood up, began shouting and banging his fist on a table, and waving a letter over his head.

"Damn Germans didn't learn anything from the Great War! Now they've executed some University of Munich students!"

"Calm down, Ben," said Professor Sol Rozinsky, who leaped up to restrain him.

"Just for speaking out... that's all they did... just for speaking out! How can I calm down? My nephew is a student there...his father is sick with worry... he wrote this from Berlin... read it... read it... go on."

Professor Rozinsky grabbed the letter and looked at it.

"It's those *brownshirts,* headed up by that Herman Goering goon, and that Austrian corporal, Adolf Hitler," said Professor Alexander Goldfarb.

Several chimed in.

"The National Socialists are out to wreck Germany."

"Nazis are swastika-wearing criminals."

"Hitler got elected only because of Hindenberg's age."

"Ha ha ha. That's simple enough."

"Von Papen could have held him off… piss ant."

"Germany's economy is as weak as ours."

"Hitler promised to support free enterprise, restrain the communists and the trade unions."

"That's why they voted for that rabble-rouser."

"Industry and the business sector supported Hitler. They expect him to fail … then back to the aristocracy."

"Dah-de-dah-de-dah."

"With a descendant of the Kaiser."

"How can glory and privilege return after jackbooted thugs?"

"Listen to this," said Professor Rozinsky. He read aloud from the letter. 'Since September 28, Jews have been banned from all cultural and entertainment activities, including literature, art, film and theater…' Can you imagine that? But it goes on. '… even prohibited from being journalists. All German newspapers have been shut down, or put under Nazi control…'"

*   *   *

February 1934

Hollywood

Torrential rain pounded the roof of the limousine as it idled inside the studio gate. Jane's chauffeur awaited a signal from the security guard to venture slowly onto the drenched street. Several limousines queued up behind. For three days a Pacific storm inundated Southern California, creating axle-deep pools of water at intersections and lowlands.

Jane was fatigued. The hour was midnight. To stay within Jack Wagner's aggressive production schedule, three motion picture crews were working late. She'd just finished a scene showing her escaping down a rope ladder from a castle tower.

What fun, she thought, getting the script changed. Originally, the scene showed Robin Hood rescuing Maid Marian from the tower. Jane reasoned that her character could be made stronger if she wasn't simply a *damsel in distress*. Why not let her escape from the tower without assistance?

"Robin Hood would be attracted to a resourceful, organized woman?" she said.

Jack Wagner concurred, then changed the title from *Robin Hood* to *Maid Marian & Robin Hood*.

"Jane is the American star of the film," he said.

"A lady just got out of the limo behind us, Miss Palmer," said the chauffeur, gazing into his rear view mirror. Raindrops obscured the windows. "Can't make her out ... she's running this way."

The door opened beside Jane. A drenched brunette leaned in.

"Hi, Doll," she said. "We need to talk. Mind if I ride with you? I live in Santa Monica."

"You're dripping wet, Ruby," replied Jane. "Get in."

Ruby Stevens was starring in *Annie Oakley.*

"I'll let the other driver know," said the chauffeur, as he exited with an umbrella.

"Klaus has become the talk of the town," said Ruby. "The press is doing what it does best…selling papers."

"Invented nonsense," replied Jane. "That's what it is."

Ruby removed a mirror and handkerchief from her purse. "Am I a sight or what? These braids come with the role."

"And shooting holes through silver dollars, I hear."

"Ha ha ha. Straight shootin' is my aim, Doll. Gotta stay in character... it's all theater, you know."

The chauffeur returned. "We've got the signal to go," he said. "Miss Palmer... Studio City, *then* Santa Monica?"

"Good plan, Ruby?" asked Jane.

"Through rain or shine," she replied.

Lightning fragmented the night sky, followed by claps of thunder. The windows fogged up as the downpour gained intensity.

"Sounds of a hundred centipedes tap-dancing on the roof," shouted the chauffeur.

"We've got a budding writer in our midst," said Ruby.

"This would be a snow blizzard in Chicago," replied Jane. She leaned forward to be heard.

Ruby moved close and whispered. "I threw myself at Klaus, Doll."

Jane stiffened, but didn't change her expression. Ruby gripped her arm with both hands.

"Others have, too," she said. "Talk about being summarily dismissed...he was nice about it... charming is the right word... to the others, too. Word gets around. One had a fit. She told me all about it in an absolute rage."

Jane began to respond, but Ruby placed a finger on her lips.

"Klaus is one in a million, Doll," she whispered. "All he talks about is you. Faithfulness is rare in this town."

Chapter Nine

LINCOLN, NEBRASKA

Hundreds of migrants queued up in multiple lines for the hot meal being served across the street from City Hall. They'd lost their farms, homes, jobs, savings, and way of life. Every week the faces were different, but despair was ever-present.

Kenny served mashed potatoes and gravy, while Darrell Cassidy cut and portioned out the meat. They'd worked side-by-side every Sunday for a year. Teddy's shifts were Wednesdays—her only day off from the hospital.

Thousands volunteered throughout America.

Roads were crowded with aged vehicles and canvas-covered wagons, filled with belongings and family members, headed anywhere over the horizon that offered hope and renewed dignity. Tent cities sprang up in hundreds of locales.

"Where you headed," Kenny asked occasionally.

"Chasin' the rainbow," was a common reply.

Trains added empty flatcars and unlocked boxcars to accommodate them. Migrants shared with each other. Strangers discussed destinations and job prospects.

A fraternity brother appeared and handed a telegram to Darrell.

"It just arrived," he said.

Darrell stepped away from the food table to read it.

"I've been accepted!" he shouted. "I've been accepted!"

He knelt and pounded the ground with both hands in pure joy. The food line stopped. Everybody watched.

"Look at this, Kenny," he shouted. "Read it! I applied for Navy Officer Candidate School. I've been accepted! I report to Newport, Rhode Island, on August first.

* * *

Two weeks later

Kenny strode from his apartment to the baccalaureate ceremony on campus. It was only three blocks away. He'd receive his PhD degree within the hour. Teddy left earlier to save seats for family members and friends from Chicago and Dalton.

Two months earlier, unbeknownst to Kenny, Dr. Hellman had mailed copies of his doctoral thesis to selected scientists and government agencies. Kenny had shown the final draft to Teddy. She'd politely *acted* interested.

"It's interesting, Honey," she said.

So is a garbage truck in a parade, he thought. Or an elephant wearing a girdle. He'd invented a two-word reply to the repetitive question, "What's your thesis about?"

"*Code breaking.*"

"Oh," was a frequent reply. And, "I see."

Hieroglyphics and *gobbledygook* were common characterizations by the uninformed about his chosen topic.

As he approached the campus gate, a chauffeured limousine stopped alongside him. A well-dressed, owlish-looking man with extraordinarily large eyes emerged.

"Mr. Kroneldt, I've been waiting for you," he said, with a British accent.

He handed over his card. It read:

Alastair Denniston
Operations-GC&CS, MI6, London.

"I'm familiar with your excellent work," he said. "Hellman and Auerbach have kept me informed. Yours is a gift that could influence the outcome of a future event. My government is working on a mathematics-based research project, and assembling a team to work with me on it. I'm the Assistant Director."

He got in the limousine and rolled down the window.

"I'll be in touch before certain developments occur," he said. "Your position here is secure until then."

The limousine sped away.

*   *   *

Jane didn't know what to say.

Seated beside Klaus on the sound stage for their third film together, *The Priest's Redemption*, she'd been studying her lines for the last scene.

"My father has asked me to return to Germany," whispered Klaus.

She could only stare at him.

"Adolph Hitler's National Socialist government has kept my father's factory busy with plenty of contracts… even helped him hire new managers."

"Why do you need to be there?" asked Jane.

"I've convinced him that I won't abandon acting."

"Why then?"

"The new government is dedicated to the arts like never before. Millions of *reichmarks* have been appropriated. They asked my father to contact me about appearing in films produced by the state."

"Features?"

"What else? Germans are suffering through the prolonged economic crisis, just like here in America. The government's goals are to foster national pride… portray the Fatherland in its true light… display normalcy."

"That's from your parents?"

"The Interior Minister. Father sent me his letter."

"Artists and scientists are fleeing Germany…"

"Disloyal ones, pretending not to understand."

"…by the hundreds?"

"Propaganda, Jane, that's all it is. The true number is little more than a handful. Hollywood propagandizes, too. You and I have been victimized by that ourselves."

"Clive and Mr. Wagner have talked to Marlene Dietrich about a picture with me, Klaus. She's one who fled Germany."

How can we know the real reasons why anyone does anything?"

"How soon will you return?" Jane wiped a tear from her cheek. Klaus held her in his arms.

"I love you, Jane. Marry me…come with me."

Jane felt dizzy. Her vision blurred. She struggled loose from him, and ran tearfully to her dressing room.

She yearned to run away with Klaus— to Hawaii or Carmel or Victoria or Bermuda or Key West— anywhere but Germany. She loved him. For months, she'd waited for him to state his intentions.

Now, a new paradox: how could she endure being separated from him? But, how could she accompany him to Germany?

* * *

One week later

The Burbank airport was virtually empty after midnight. A chartered airplane was booked for one passenger—Klaus Leonhardt. From New York, he'd board a freighter bound for Bremerhaven, German—then on to Berlin.

Klaus embraced Jane at the gate. They'd promised to keep the marriage proposal a secret.

"I love you, Jane. Don't worry. I'll be back soon."

"I'll marry you when you return."

* * *

Two weeks later, his letters began to arrive. He'd begun his starring role in a film entitled, *Lebensraum*.

"The government producer makes daily script changes—sometimes entire scenes are added or torn out," he wrote. "He argues with the director in front of the cast—even allows outside government officials to view the rushes every day."

Jane had begun filming, *Cocktails For Two*, a comedy about two nightclub singers competing for one suitor. She co-starred with Marlene Dietrich and Ronald Colman. The two actresses spent much time together, on and off the set. Jane soon regarded Marlene her German mentor.

"Adolf Hitler will use his distortion of *Lebensraum* to hold the world hostage," said Marlene Dietrich during a late-night supper. "Wait and see."

"It's a film," replied Jane. "Just entertainment."

"Ha ha ha. Propaganda posing as entertainment. How does Klaus describe it?"

"He plays a farmer… protecting his land near the German border from being taken over by foreigners."

"How does he do that?"

"He repels the first raiders, single-handedly… then recruits other farmers."

"I assume he becomes the leader."

"Of course. He organizes citizens from nearby towns."

"Let me guess… they form a militia …"

"And cooperate with local police and army officials."

"Ha ha ha. Who are the foreigners?"

"Gypsies, Jews from Austria, Poland, Czechoslavakia."

" … all played as devils."

"Klaus deals with constant treachery. It's very dramatic. He loves the role."

"Ha ha ha. Has he told you what *Lebensraum* means?"

"Isn't it a search for unity between land and people?"

"Hitler's euphemism for *blood and soil.* That's why I left Germany."

"I don't understand."

"Hitler is re-defining *Lebensraum.* Its literal translation is 'opening up living space within Germany.' He claims it is overcrowded with undesirables, who need to be eliminated. He's already begun removing Jews from their homes to unknown destinations, and confiscating their property and businesses. It will get much worse."

"How is that possible?"

"We exiles believe he will contrive a political reason for annexing bordering countries, by force if necessary, depriving those people of their lands...re-populating them with Germanic people. That's the new living space... Adolf Hitler's revision of *Lebensraum.*"

"Where will they go? Hitler would never get away with it... how could he?"

Marlene Dietrich shrugged. "What you've told me about Klaus's film proves that Hitler's campaign has already begun."

* * *

U.S. Embassy, London
October 19, 1935

Dear Jane;

Being the military attaché's aide here at the Embassy has kept me hopping. Travel galore. Long hours. I've met several heads-of-state, prime ministers, military brass. Much pomp, but no circumstance. I mustn't forget King George V. He's been ill, but gave the Ambassador an audience at Sandringham Palace. I got to meet him.

Your concern for Klaus Leonhardt's safety is noted. You sound like you are taken with him. It's true that the German government has been shaking things up, but is primarily what the military and European politicians refer to as saber-rattling—against internal, political dissenters and criminal-types. The English military hasn't shown concern, nor has any other European country that we are aware of. Keep in mind, Germany is hosting the 1936 Olympics. They want to make a good impression on visitors by removing proven troublemakers.

The economy throughout Europe is similar to that of the U.S —bad . We've learned, however, that German factories are functioning at a considerably higher level than those in other European countries. England, by comparison, is far below norms. Father deserves a great deal of credit by arranging for his hotels to be debt-free before the market crashed.

Good news! There's lines at theaters to see my little sister's films. Everyone in the Embassy is a Jane Palmer fan. The Ambassador, too. He

constantly asks me about you. Send more signed
photos. I'm all out.

Love and kisses from your proud stepbrother,

George

Maj. George Fisher

*

Fisher Hotel
Chicago, Illinois

October 26, 1935

Dearest Jane;

Your step-father and I wish we were there
to comfort you more. You have been through so
much this year. We hope you are not overdoing
it. When you finish your picture, please come
home for awhile. Why don't you ask Jack Wagner
to schedule the premiere in Chicago? Adrian is
willing to sponsor a premiere party here at the
hotel.

George wrote that he would assure you about
Klaus Leonhardt. He assured us that your handsome beau has nothing to worry about.

Not only that—we are well-acquainted with hotel people around the world, including Berlin. Hoteliers share ideas for guest services and operations. Louis and Hedda Lorenz own the Adlon Hotel in Berlin where Klaus is staying. It and the Regent are the city's finest. Louis replied to Adrian's query that every room is booked, future prospects look good, Hitler has promised to stabilize the economy. The expanded police presence that you have expressed concern about helps to protect business interests and, of course, banks and citizens.

Love,

Mother

Chapter Ten

Three days each week Kenny lunched with a small group of professors in the Student Union Building cafeteria. Conversations covered a wide range of current issues. They joked that, "if world leaders would only listen to us… ha ha ha."

A clerk from the campus post office across the hall spotted Kenny, and delivered a package to his table. It was clearly marked, *Official Business - British Government Mail.*

He opened it. The package contained a hand-written letter and official documents marked, *Declassified.* His tablemates watched him thumb through the contents and peruse the letter.

"'… recent European events have hastened the importance and timeliness of …,'" he finally read softly, seemingly to himself.

"You've piqued my curiosity," said Professor Rozinsky.

"Ditto," said Professor Goldfarb.

"It may be a private matter," said Professor Hellman.

"Government isn't private, Mo," replied Rozinsky.

"'*Recent European events*' can only mean one thing," said Professor Cohen, "Hitler and his gang of thugs."

"Did you hear how the Gestapo got its name?" asked Hellman.

"Changing the subject won't prevent Kenny from telling us what this is all about," said Rozinsky.

"It's from Alastair Denniston," replied Kenny. "He works for some sort of secret agency in England. I do not know its name, only its initials. I met him briefly on graduation day. Have any of you met him?"

All but Hellman shook their heads.

"Auerbach and I spoke with Denniston about you at great length that week," replied Hellman. "He focused on your math prowess."

"I didn't know," replied Kenny.

"A formality of his inquiry," said Hellman.

"Oooh… aura of mystery," said Rozinsky. "This is getting better and better."

"It's declassified," said Kenny. "I'll read it."

Professor Hellman nodded.

*

Dear Dr. Kroneldt;

I wish to familiarize you to the mission of my agency and provide insight into the rapid progress of cryptography in recent years.

The yellow folder contains cipher texts and a *key*. I wish to challenge you to decrypt its contents within twenty-four hours of receipt and return to me. It is elemental in cryptographic terms— dating back to the Great War. We have advanced the science light years since. Cryptography roots pre-date Julius Caesar. He utilized transposition and substitution ciphers. Most people could not read in those days, so its simplicity was adequate. Think Boolean algebra.

In any event, each fortnight I plan to mail you a package (exponentially more difficult) and invite your accommodation. Recent European events have hastened the importance and timeliness of your future involvement.

Respectfully submitted,

Alastair Denniston
Operations - GC&CS, MI-6
London

*

Kenny looked up at them when he finished.

"Sounds like derring-do of high order," said Goldfarb.

"How do you think we know so much about that rotten Hitler, for God's sake?" asked Cohen.

"Espionage, that's how," said Rozinsky.

"The German's can't start anything after their humiliating defeat in the Great War," said Goldfarb. "They wouldn't dare."

"Ha ha ha, that's good," said Cohen. "Adolph Hitler wants to keep Jews out of the Olympics... he's established a concentration camp in Dachau for dissidents... he's created a secret police force... and most recently, his *Gestapo Law*."

"What's that?" asked Goldfarb.

"It shelters any actions by the Gestapo from any administrative court," replied Hellman.

"Meaning… that the Gestapo is above the law," said Cohen. "There's no legal appeal regarding whatever it does."

"But, Germany is a democracy," replied Goldfarb.

It's conceivable," said Hellman, "that anyone can be arrested, interrogated, and sent to a concentration camp for incarceration or execution without any legal procedure."

"When did that happen?" asked Goldfarb.

"Last week," replied Hellman.

"That is most likely the *recent events*, referred to in Denniston's letter," said Rozinsky.

"The Gestapo has come a law upon itself," said Hellman.

"Such an odd word… Gestapo," said Rozinsky. "Is that German?"

"One of Hitler's henchmen, Hermann Goering, created the Secret Police Office shortly after Hitler was elected Chancellor," replied Hellman. "Its initials were *GPA*. Then the name was changed to *Secret State Police*, which in German is *Geheime Staats Polizei*. One day, a postal clerk abbreviated a label on a mailbag being delivered to them, and simply wrote *Ge-Sta-Po*. It stuck."

"Horrible sounding," said Cohen. "Simply horrible."

* * *

My Dearest Jane,

I'm aching to be back in your arms. I'm limited to gazing at your photograph every night in my hotel room, at my table during meals, on the set, everywhere I go.

Berlin is groomed for the Olympics. The whole world will be impressed. The stadium and various venues are truly magnificent! Entire sections of the city have been rehabilitated with new storefronts, signs, street repairs, lighting, many new shop-owners. Police and soldiers are everywhere to assure a smooth visit for hundreds of thousands of tourists.

I hear marching practice every night in the street below my hotel window. Well-dressed shoppers fill the streets in their elegant dresses, parasols, fashionable hats, veils. You would love it here.

About the film: My character, Franz, organizes a militia. Thousands of patriots volunteer. He's wounded in a battle, but fights on. They beat back the interlopers, and save Germany. In a huge crowd scene (final act), the Chancellor promotes him to the rank of Colonel.

Father could not come to Berlin. He wired me that the plant is keeping him too busy.

Lebensraum is booked for the entire two weeks of the Olympics at every theater in Germany. A publicity campaign is planned. Gigantic posters of me will be everywhere—as a farmer and militia Colonel.

My return to California will be delayed. Public appearance commitments will require that I stay for a time when the Olympics end. After that, we will share our lives together.

Love as ever,

Klaus

* * *

Kenny's first decryption took fifteen minutes to solve. The second and third mailing took longer, but he'd familiarized himself with the folders contents, and confidently deciphered the coded messages as easily as completing the *New York Times* crossword puzzle. The first message read:

> *Solve in less than one hour and you are way ahead of the game. Britain leads in cryptography. Mathematics is the future of the science. See Auerbach after you mail decryption from third package.*

* * *

"Cryptography allows us to have eyes and ears in the enemy camp," said Dr. Auerbach.

He and Kenny occupied a café booth six blocks from campus. For thirty minutes, the University president explained his support for code-breaking and espionage.

"Why not be involved with the U.S. version?" asked Kenny.

"We have no version," replied Auerbach. "Only inter-service rivalries... distance from the Great War battlefields... peacetime mentality... old-school military philosophies... resistance to change... profound ignorance of reality."

"My sister's stepbrother is a military attaché in the U.S. Embassy, London, and he told her ..."

"That Hitler is simply keeping order within Germany's borders... that it's an *internal housekeeping matter*. Garbage! That's what it is."

"Isn't he in a good position to..."

"One would think so, but the current consensus of European nations is that Russia's Stalin presents a more plausible threat to world order and peace than does the vanquished and crippled Germany, stripped in 1918 of its air force and U-boats, and limited by the Versailles Treaty to a small army. Baron Von Hindenberg appeared to be honoring that, but he's dead."

"Does the *current consensus* include England?"

"Yes, but not the project that Denniston is developing. He's operating between the cracks, so to speak."

"Can't America do the same?"

"Ha ha ha. What do we teach in American history? The Constitution... the Bill of Rights... civil liberties... equal rights. The British have a broader sense of bureaucratic form and fewer constitutional barriers to the legal suspension of civil liberties. They simply pass legislation that gives government the power to read cables and private mail, regardless of who they're to or from."

"What he sent me was easy."

"Of course. You are *you*... Dr. Kenneth Palmer Kroneldt, PhD... gifted prodigy of mathematics and physics. Nobody else is like you. You're a phenomenon, Kenny. When are you going to get that through your head? Denniston didn't send you the hard stuff. Nobody can decipher the hard stuff. That's why they want you."

"Are they all mathematicians?"

"Very few. Some are historians, linguists, classicists. They share a single-minded focus and a scholar's aptitude for piecing together perplexity into coherency."

"How do you know Alastair Denniston?"

"An Oxford connection. Academia is a close group."

"It's odd you're recruiting for him."

"You're a feather in our cap, Kenny. I'll arrange to list you as faculty on paid leave at ten percent of your current salary to augment whatever they offer."

"Even if I cannot send you any information?"

"That's a given. Perhaps a book when you return."

"Are you familiar with code-breaking and espionage?"

"*Impenetrable* is my word for it."

"What if I can't?"

"Ha ha ha. Of course you can. It's a numbers game, Kenny. Don't you teach that any numbers theory created by mathematicians can be solved by mathematicians?"

"Random numbers may be the challenge."

"It's rumored the Germans have developed a machine."

"No one's told me."

"You need to get involved."

"Move to England with Teddy?"

"Denniston is prepared to offer you a position there. Teddy can't be left out. Qualified operating room nurses are in great demand. He will arrange for her certification. Following spring semester would be the right time."

* * *

It wasn't easy for Jane to open the mail box every day, for weeks on end, and find no letter from Klaus.

Two months had elapsed since his last one. None of her own were returned. George Fisher wrote only that *Lebensraum* was popular in German theaters. Newspaper columnists speculated that he'd returned to German cinema. Louis Adlon wired Adrian Fisher that Klaus departed his hotel three days after the Olympics—accompanied by four Nazi soldiers. A reporter confronted Jane in the studio commissary, where she shared a lunch table with Marlene Dietrich.

"Miss Palmer, Klaus Leonhardt vacated his Sunset Strip bungalow," he said. "Were you aware of that?"

"Do ladies usually get asked such questions?"

"The manager there told me this morning two men with German accents showed up last week with written permission to remove his personal belongings... then did."

"Was it his signature?" asked Marlene.

"I compared it to the one on his rental contract."

"What about his car?" asked Jane.

"That's what put me onto this story. His Bugatti was consigned to a dealership in San Francisco, then sold to an Oregon buyer."

"I wish I knew something," said Jane.

"He's already missed one picture assignment with her," said Marlene. "She cannot tell you what she does not know."

"Mr. Wagner appears unconcerned. Shouldn't he be?"

"Ha ha ha... now you are trying to get us into trouble with the boss," replied Marlene. "Such a question can only be asked of him. You obviously already have."

"Where do you *think* Klaus Leonhardt might be, Miss Palmer?" asked the reporter.

"His parents own a factory in Schrobenhausen, near Munich," replied Jane.

"Not anymore."

"What do you mean?"

"The Nazis have nationalized the factories throughout Germany, according to reports out of Poland. Klaus Leonhardt's family has dropped out of sight."

Chapter Eleven

Kenny's first fortnight in London was a rudimentary introduction to code-making, code-breaking and espionage—and to the secret nature of the organization he was joining.

The first document he signed was a copy of Britain's *Official Secrets Act*, which prevented him from disclosing his involvement to anyone—including family members—outside the agency. Consequences were characterized as perilous to one's well-being, freedom, and country.

"What we decipher, encipher, ferret out of the woodwork… and how we go about it," intoned Dennison, "mandates a very narrow circle of distribution."

It had been a lonely, week-long journey crossing the Atlantic by passenger liner for Kenny, who'd left Teddy behind for his indoctrination. Alastair Denniston met him at dockside early in the morning, expedited him through customs, then drove him into the city—pointing out shortcuts, principal arterials, tram stops, and various eating and drinking establishments.

The Broadway Buildings, located opposite St. James tube station, housed GC&CS offices, and were around the corner from the Foreign Office. Denniston parked in a small, gated lot, two blocks distant.

"You won't need an automobile this trip," he said. "You're sharing a flat with a chap, Alan Turing. Right across the street… short walk." He pointed to a four-story brick building in the middle of the block—the Viceroy Hotel. A sign read: *Weekly and monthly rates*. "Turing's your age… arrived two days ago… an Englishman, but born in India … mathematical genius like yourself… educated at Princeton… not far from Nebraska, eh? …leave your bags… we'll get you checked-in after lunch."

As they approached the building entrance, Denniston gripped Kenny's arm. "Always walk past it," he whispered, "then around the corner to the Foreign Office entry when you're with a non-associate. You never want anyone to know where you work. Bid them goodbye… see them off… count to 120… then return here. When you board the lift, simply say 'third'… never the agency name. There's other offices and visitors in the building, you see."

"My sister's stepbrother works at the U.S. Embassy and…" said Kenny.

"No exceptions, lad. Never."

Kenny peered across the busy street at the narrow stairway leading down to the tube station, and the signage that identified it. It reminded him of subway entries in Chicago, where he'd lived as a young boy before his parents died.

"'C' wants to meet you," said Denniston. "He's expecting us at the Foreign Office."

* * *

The corridor on the fourth floor of the Foreign Office contained many doors on each side with opaque glass and generic
signing, such as *Library, Secretary Pool, Incoming, Outgoing, Conference, Small Conference,* and *Wash Room.* The door leading to
their destination was unmarked, except for the room number, 426.
As Denniston and Kenny entered, the receptionist said brightly,
"I'm willing to wager you are Dr. Kroneldt from America."

"Correct, as you always are, Mrs. Pemberton," replied Denniston. "Dr. Kenneth Palmer Kroneldt from the University of Nebraska, USA, and the fine little hamlet of Dalton, Nebraska, to be
precise. May I introduce Mrs. Pemberton, the keeper of the gate,
and fortune-teller deluxe, I might add. 'C' is a lucky man to have
such a protector, indeed."

Kenny smiled, took her hand, and kissed it. "I, as well, surmised you are the indefatigable Mrs. D. Pemberton."

"A real charmer, aren't you," she replied, as she turned the
nameplate on her desk upside down. "My crystal ball tells me
you're both here to see the Director."

"Half right," replied Denniston.

"What half am I missing?" asked Mrs. Pemberton.

"That 'C' will be here to see us?"

"Ha, such jocularity. Sit… be a good boy." She turned toward
double oak doors leading into 'C's inner sanctum, just as a light
above the molding turned green. "Never mind. He's ready for you
now."

Kenny first noticed the bowler hat on the clothes tree inside
the door, then the silver-handled cane, and finally the gray-haired,
bespectacled, balding man, seated behind an enormous, mahogany desk in the spacious office that contained a fireplace, book
shelves on three walls, two sofas, and leather chairs.

Kenny had previously been informed by Denniston that 'C' was a retired admiral and the former Director of Naval Intelligence, who'd been brought in to the Foreign Office several years earlier to head up the Secret Intelligence Service (SIS)—also known as MI6— and Government Code & Cypher School (GC&CS). His name was Hugh 'Quex' Sinclair. 'C's predecessor was Mansfield Cummings, who'd originated the single letter designation. Admiral Sinclair chose to avoid confusion by not changing it to 'Q' or 'S' when he took over.

"Got any aces up your sleeve?" he asked, after the two visitors seated themselves, following introduction pleasantries. "I'm aware of your gambling skills. I didn't have a professor your age at Cambridge, did you, Denniston?"

"Youth is taking over, no question," he replied.

'C' offered cigars from a crocodile skin-covered case on his desk. Both turned him down. He removed one, bit off the tip, casually lit it, and exhaled smoke rings.

"We're here because we need to know what's going on in Germany," he said. He leaned back in his chair. "We don't know as much as we'd like, Kroneldt. That's why you're here."

Silence followed, as 'C' puffed on his cigar and blew out more smoke rings.

"We've got the American, Italian, and French diplomatic codes down pat," he said, "as though they originated during the Crusades, lazy blokes. The Poles... you've got to hand it to them... as you will see... have re-created a version of the German's Enigma machine without even seeing one. We have it. They gave it to us. Turing is tinkering with it now. Three rotors... that's what it has. That creates the odds of more than 17,000 to 1 to select their current code-setting. They keep changing it. Diabolical bastards. You know the number precisely, don't you Denniston?"

"17,576… the number is carved on my brain…but we've developed and recognize *cribs* to get it down to more manageable size," he replied.

"That requires days… sometimes weeks or more… many times dead ends… even with your *cribs*. Compare the German yesteryear's codes to today's for Kroneldt, similar to how you briefed Turing two days ago."

"Think of a code book, Professor," said Denniston, "containing thousands of five-letter or five-digit code-groups, each representing a letter, word, phrase… with a simple substitution for each one in a message. That was Germany's encryption method yesteryear… even preceding the Great War. Much like tiptoeing through tulips, but deciphered with careful analysis, focus, and determination. England's future… the world's future… was at stake. Our challenge then, as it is now, was taking action using the information that we gathered, so that we did not tip off the Germans that we'd broken their code. Otherwise, they would have constantly changed their code book. That's why the information must be so closely held. Sharing, even between agencies, is a risk.

"Today, all that has changed. There's still a book with code-groups, but each one is added to a series of letters or digits selected from a second book, containing thousands more. Then, each code-group is enciphered with a varied substitution method. Finally, the entire message is treated to one more such manipulation… meaning, a sequence of additives, drawn from a different starting point in the second book, is added to the message.

"Your job with Alan Turing and other mathematicians, as yet not recruited, will be to develop the know-how to recognize changes in the Enigma machine-settings. We need the ability to decipher intercepted messages within minutes of their receipt… not days or weeks. It's clear to a few of us in the British government that the Germans are up to no good. Are you game for the challenge?"

"How are the machine-settings discovered?" asked Kenny.

"Painstaking analysis of hundreds of messages… eighty, minimum," replied Denniston, "comparison of cipher repetitions, common headings, lazy senders, mathematical logic, length, stealth, espionage, luck."

"Will you repeat the 17,000 number," asked Kenny.

"17,576."

Kenny wrote a calculation on the palm of his hand. 'C' and Denniston waited.

"I see how you arrived at it," said Kenny.

"At what?" asked Denniston.

"When you mentioned, 'comparison of cipher repetitions and common headings', which I deduce comprise part of your definition of '*cribs*', and that the German Enigma machine contains three rotors, your number makes sense. Tell me if I'm correct. The alphabet has twenty-six letters. Each of the three rotors contains twenty-six gear teeth, representing the alphabet. Each rotor is independent of the other two. The operator sets them at random. 17,576 is 26 to the third power… in other words, 26 times 26 times 26. Therefore, there are 17,576 possible 3-letter combinations, with those givens. However, thousands of those can be eliminated outright. For example, a majority of consonants don't go together, such as gf and tk. Those that do, more frequently than not, pair a consonant with a vowel. Another example… reciprocals are what they are. They work both ways. If f equals s, then s equals f. If b equals v, then v equals b…and so on through the alphabet. Reciprocals, alone, reduce the possibilities by half. My guess is that the real number would be considerably less than one-fourth, plus or minus. More likely, less than a fifth or sixth."

"I look forward to your working with us, Dr. Kroneldt," said 'C'. "We hope to move GC&CS and MI6 out of London. It's growing. We're driving to Bletchley in Buckinghamshire tomorrow morning to take a look at a prospective site. Care to go?"

* * *

Kenny knew he'd like Alan Turing, shortly after he met him on the third floor of the Broadway Buildings. Holding a piece of chalk, Turing stood alone, wearing sandals and t-shirt, in a small, windowless room. Furnishings consisted of two metal chairs and a small table, upon which sat a pile of documents and an odd-looking machine with typewriter keys. Mathematical formulae covered blackboards on four walls. Wadded-up paper covered the floor.

Although twenty-five years old, Turing appeared ten years younger, with effeminate mannerisms. His light brown hair, combed straight back, exposed an enormous forehead and an openness of self-presentation that accompanied an engaging smile and unkempt apparel.

"I believe I'm on to something," he said, as Kenny and Denniston entered.

"Alan Turing, I want you to meet your new associate, Dr. Kenneth Kroneldt, from America."

"Give me a moment," he replied, as he leaned down, picked up a crumpled piece of paper, unfolded it, gave it a cursory look, wadded it up, dropped it, picked up another, smoothed it out, completed the equation on the blackboard, then turned to face them. "The pleasure is all mine, Kenneth," he said as he offered his hand. "I'm Alan Turing. I heard all about you at Princeton. Now, here we are together in the middle of a riddle, eh?"

"One that's constantly evolving," replied Kenny.

"The Enigma rotors are compelling elements."

Kenny peered at the machine on the table and ran his hand over its gold-colored gears. "Which way do they rotate?"

"Clockwise."

"Looking from inside or outside the machine?"

"Ha ha ha. Good show, Kroneldt," exclaimed Denniston. "That's the kind of thinking that'll expand our bounds. What say we lunch together, get the professor checked into the hotel, then commence your indoctrination, and bring you up-to-date on the challenges."

*   *   *

Kenny had not anticipated riding in an open Lancia Touring Car to Bletchley, but early the following morning 'C' appeared with his own in front of the Viceroy Hotel, where Kenny and Alan Turing stood waiting.

"Let the lads take turns riding up front," hollered 'C', as Denniston exited the vehicle and motioned Turing to follow him into the spacious rear seat—allowing Kenny to sit next to the Director.

'C' pulled away from the curb as the doors closed and weaved the vehicle skillfully through morning traffic—waving jauntily to staring pedestrians. After several minutes of winding streets, unexpected maneuvers, and accelerations, he turned onto A-5, the road heading northwesterly out of London.

"Like the wind in your hair?" he asked Kenny.

"I've been riding my Harley-Davidson for years," replied Kenny. "Nothing like it."

"Does it have right hand drive? Ha ha ha... it appears I'm the first to ask you that, eh?"

Kenny's eyes widened. Alan Turing leaned into the conversation from the rear seat.

"My sources indicate that no American-made motorcycle has right hand drive, Director," he said. "Ha ha ha."

"Puts a crimp in their *rightful* export prospects, wouldn't you think?" asked Denniston. "Ha ha ha."

"And without Britain as a trade partner, who's *left*?" asked Turing.

"Right!" replied Kenny.

Everyone laughed.

"Denniston," said 'C', looking over his shoulder, "I'm confident Kroneldt can improvise. See to it that his Harley-Davidson motorcycle gets shipped over with his belongings."

"Good as done," replied Denniston, "but, he'll need to avoid the right side of the road. Ha ha ha."

"It's only the right thing to do," replied Kenny. "After all... what other side is left?"

Everyone laughed. Silence fell over the group for several minutes, as the Lancia motored through the suburbs against inbound traffic. 'C' relit his cigar. A train full of commuters sped toward London on tracks parallel to the road. Bright sun had broken through the cloud cover, providing Kenny with a panoramic view of the English landscape—stone houses abutting assorted shoppes, spans of rolling meadows, hedgerows, occasional walled estates, then more stone houses.

"Teddington is straight ahead," said 'C'. "I need to check on one of my properties."

He reduced speed through the town plaza, passed the train station and hospital, then turned onto Grove Terrace Road, and stopped beside a brick townhouse. A sign in the yard read, 'To Let-Furnished'.

"Your bride may find this quite suitable, Kroneldt," said 'C'. "It's a twenty-five minute commute to the St. James tube station... less on your Harley-Davidson. Care to take a look?"

*   *   *

Kenny rode in the rear seat beside Denniston for the thirty minute drive from Teddington to Bletchley, following the house tour. He needed to lean forward to hear 'C', who talked about geography and biography along the way.

"Think of a giant capital T," he said, "consisting of a ten foot post and four foot crossbar flat on the ground. The foot of the T faces southeast... that's London. Teddington is just short of midway along the post. The crossbar mid-point is Bletchley, a small town in Buckinghamshire in the Borough of Milton Keynes. The long post represents A-5, the road we're on. It's also the train route for the *West Coast Main Line* from London that continues on past Bletchley all the way to Scotland. The crossbar connects Oxford and Cambridge, southwest to northeast. A different train provides service between the two Universities. When I was an undergraduate at Cambridge, we referred to it as 'the brain train.' Its real name is *Varsity Line*.

"After college," asked Kenny, "did you feel destined to become an admiral in the Royal Navy?"

"My father and grandfather were admirals. It was my career path from the outset. Family tradition is weighty in Britain's military."

"Your grandfather might be astounded at the changes."

"My father, too. Sailing ships have become tourist artifacts... sailors are called seamen... coal's been replaced by oil... navigation systems mechanized. And intelligence-gathering? Ha ha ha.

"When the Great War began, Naval reconnaissance was a ship peeking into enemy harbors. Some were met with cannon broadsides. The First Lord of the Admiralty, Winston Churchill, ordered the practice stopped in 1914, but before his order was carried out, a German submarine torpedoed three cruisers on slow patrol at Dogger Bank in the middle of the North Sea. Fourteen-hundred sailors drowned."

"Heavy costs for progress and freedom," said Turing.

"Ditto, learning and change," said Denniston.

"Notable resistance to change remains," replied 'C', "in government and military circles to what we're about... even why we are necessary. It's peacetime, they say. There can be no more wars, they proclaim. Stiff-arming change, whatever one's endeavor, is the nature of the human beast. The few of us press on... like moving elephants through hardening rubber."

Kenny's first view of their destination looked like four fraternity and sorority houses crammed together—each with its own architectural style—to become a single residence. The two-story Victorian-Tudor-Dutch Baroque conglomeration sat in the middle of a fifty-five acre grassy, well-treed, piece of ground amidst several out-buildings. North Road bordered it on the front—just a couple of turns off A-5.

"When Sir Herbert Leon bought this property in 1883," said 'C', "the prior owner had already named the estate Bletchley Park." He steered past the open iron gate onto an imposing, oval-shaped driveway. "His widow died recently. If you are confronted with cheeky questions, we are Captain Ridley's hunting party."

Chapter Twelve

Jane sat beside Marlene Dietrich, Jack Wagner, and Clive Rogel in the tiny—otherwise empty—studio theater that was used primarily to view daily rushes of that day's filming. Closing titles flashed on the screen for Klaus Leonhardt's picture, *Lebensraum*, which Wagner had requested from the German studio boss several months earlier—a practice between film companies that utilized each other's principal actors. No English was spoken, nor did the production include sub-titles.

"What did I tell you," exclaimed Marlene. *"Vaterlaendischen… vaterlaendischen!* Repeated over and over and over, ad nauseum, in that utterly stupefying song at the end. *Vaterlaendischen* is German for fatherland. I refrained from losing breakfast. How gleeful they looked about their contrived triumph… kissing, hugging, holding Klaus high over their heads…looking so victorious. About what? Innocent, unlikely, fictional, interlopers from Poland and Czechoslavakia? It's all made up. Hitler will interlope them! You will see! Truth twisted upside down, inside out, a grotesque fairy tale about Nazi despots, portraying themselves as protectors, leaders, humanity's destiny for paradise and golden earrings. Eternal hell in a fiery furnace would be more fitting. How could Klaus be so naïve to get involved in it?"

"I asked about his whereabouts and doings," said Wagner. "No acknowledgment ... only the film reels. No one knows where he is."

"Maybe they simply don't know," said Clive Rogel.

"Of course they *don't* know," replied Marlene Dietrich. "Some of my Jewish friends and neighbors there have already vanished. Poof! Like that! Poof! The Nazis have learned how to hide a giraffe in a hat box."

"I want to go find him," said Jane.

"Your fate will be Klaus's if you enter Germany," replied Marlene Dietrich.

"But, they'd know me," said Jane.

"They know Klaus," replied Wagner.

"England is as close as you should get, Jane," said Clive. "I've got you booked for the starring role in *Aladdin,* at the Palladium in London during Christmas week."

*   *   *

Shipping cartons sat neatly-stacked atop a wooden foot-locker in the hallway, when Kenny and Teddy entered the Teddington residence together for the first time. Arriving at dockside on the *Queen Mary* that morning, they were greeted by a personable, Foreign Office staffer, Miss Jones, who escorted them through customs, then drove them to their new home. On the way she made various stops—including lunch—to acquaint Teddy with popular destinations.

In Teddington, they'd stopped at a bank to exchange funds and open an account, a neighborhood food market to stock up, and the local train station to pick up route maps and schedules.

"There's nowhere you can't get to from here," said Miss Jones. "You've found an ideal residence."

"How in the world did our things arrive here before we did?" asked Teddy

"England has for centuries been known for mystery, intrigue, and accomplishing the seemingly impossible, compared to the relatively-youthful United States."

"One of your former colonies," replied Kenny.

They laughed together.

Teddy had been ambivalent about leaving Nebraska and the operating room crew at Lincoln General, although she'd demonstrated wifely pride over his opportunity to work with British academia on undisclosed mathematics and physics research. She'd obtained her British nursing certification without a hitch, as promised by Dr. Auerbach, along with assurance of employment at Teddington Memorial hospital. She was scheduled to meet the chief surgeon the following afternoon.

"A reliable companion is out back," said Miss Jones, after they toured the house. She led them into the garage. Kenny's freshly-washed Harley-Davidson motorcycle awaited.

* * *

Kenny spent most of his time at GC&CS headquarters with Alan Turing. Alastair Denniston and 'C' left them alone.

Their primary tasks were testing, improving, and inventing methodologies for determining Enigma rotor-settings that cryptanalysts could utilize. German message traffic had grown precipitously in recent months.

Secondary tasks dealt with other countries' encryption systems and diplomatic codes.

German intercepts typically resembled the following extract:

BMXPZ FLCCA QPCYD EHPIG BZ-
TUN JHLAU ZADDH RXJMO TCLEI
FGWWD KXTRC QPCYD AMLDR
PDDBI ZADDH

Each of the 5-letter or digit code groups represented a single letter of the alphabet, number, word, name, ship, base, commander, location, phrase, and tens of thousands of other possibilities.

To the unpracticed eye they were hieroglyphics. The practiced eye gleaned potential weaknesses, and tested them for latent *cribs* (commonalities and clues) which, hopefully, led to solutions.

The foregoing message contained two repeated code groups— *QPCYD* and *ZADDH*. Wireless messages typically ended sentences with '*stop*'. If *ZADDH* meant '*stop*', a cryptanalyst tentatively deduced that the message consisted of two sentences, a potential *crib*—albeit a minor one. If the sentence was transposed during encryption (began in the middle, then ended with the beginning), *QPCYD* could also be a candidate for '*stop*', and the message considered to contain two sentences.

In the German language, '*eins*' meant '*and*'. Repetition of code groups flagged immediate attention from cryptanalysts. Common words and conjunctions, such as '*and*', '*from*', '*to*', '*day*', '*month*', '*title*' (such as lieutenant) were likely candidates to be repeated—particularly when culled from a group of eighty or more messages, encrypted within the previous forty-eight hours. Odds soared for a majority to have been encrypted using the same 3-letter rotor-setting.

To confound cryptanalysts, the sender used *additives*. Thus, QPCYD became UTGCH if each of the five letters in the code group advanced four steps forward in the alphabet. If they'd been advanced six steps, QPCYD would become WVIEJ, and all code groups in the message would change accordingly. If a rotor in the Enigma machine advanced by one letter, following an arbitrarily-established number of code groups, then 'stop'—or any other already-deciphered word or letter—appeared differently in a multiple-sentence message, as well as every separate message.

Kenny knew that the Germans could change the 3-rotor code setting every day if they wished. He wondered, too, when they would increase the number of rotors from three—to four or five or six or seven.

* * *

December 1937

Jane peeked through the stage curtain.

London's Palladium Theater was filled to capacity. Kenny and Teddy had front row seats. So did George Fisher and several Embassy people. All fourteen performances of *Aladdin* were sold out for her ten day engagement. There'd been only three days for rehearsals, but Jane had practiced her lines and songs during the Atlantic voyage with Hollywood friends, who'd agreed to play other roles—Lillian Lorraine as the beautiful princess; Buddy Ebsen as Hoo Flung Dat, the Emperor of China; and W.C. Fields as the Genie of the Lamp. Widow Twankey was reprised by a local history professor, who'd gained a fan base in past years.

The silly antics and improvisations of the musical provided Jane with a three-hour escape every night. She left her real persona at the stage door, and became Aladdin.

Nevertheless, British reporters hounded her about Klaus. "What if he doesn't want to be found?" asked one.

An entertainment columnist opined, "… not the first time a man broke up with his girlfriend."

Jack Wagner had reluctantly given her a letter from a studio boss in Berlin. Jane had read and re-read it so often, she needed to tape the torn creases together.

*

Jack Wagner
Wagner Studios
Hollywood, California - USA

Dear Jack;

I wish I had information to share concerning your query about the whereabouts of Klaus Leonhardt, and his parents in Schrobenhausen, but I have none. I fear the worst.

That's not all. I have been removed as studio head of *Universum Film AG* by the Minister of Propaganda, Joseph Goebbels. Other heads have rolled. Besides Herr Leonhardt, hundreds (perhaps thousands) have vanished from public view.

Since June, Germany's film industry is in the hands of *Reichsfilmkammer*, the agency created by Chancellor Hitler to control content. Already, more than 3000 film professionals (foreigners and Jews) have been barred from employment. Goebbels has recently banned film criticism and replaced it with *filmbeobachtung*—the German word for *film observation*. Reporters cannot make judgments, only write plot points that must withstand muster.

Internment camps have been set up in Dachau and Westerbork for 'dissidents'—no definition has been provided. The camps provide God-awful living conditions, I've been told. The Nazi-controlled press refers to the activity as 'improvements'. Raising the temperature in purgatory comes to mind.

I am uncertain about Germany's future, Jack. Or mine. I fear for my family's safety, as well as my own. We need to get out. Thugs rule Germany. Spread the word—every way you can.

Cross-border and overseas mail is scrutinized by censors. I cannot post this. Director Fritz Lang has booked passage for the United States next week. I have been unsuccessful doing same to date. He promised to deliver to you this letter upon his safe arrival to your shores. Pray for Klaus Leonhardt and me and our families.

May God be with all of us,

Alfred Hugenberg

* * *

Jane hardly expected to be drinking tea with England's Prime Minister Neville Chamberlain at 10 Downing Street. He'd invited her and the other Hollywood cast members—following the opening performance of *Aladdin*—two days earlier. They sat in a semicircle, facing the marble fireplace, in the elegant parlor.

"Entertainment lifts our spirits and offers a respite during these uncertain economic times," said Chamberlain.

"Jane Palmer has set a marvelous example for *recovery*," replied Lillian Lorraine. "Look at her ... good as new."

"Good show! Yes." exclaimed the Prime Minister. "Miss Palmer, you were in our prayers. You serve as a role model for overcoming grim circumstances."

"Endless bread lines in America are today's grim circumstances, Mr. Prime Minister," said Buddy Ebsen.

"I tip my hat most somberly," replied W.C. Fields.

"You've seen them here, too," replied Chamberlain. "England and America share common goals... economic recovery...maintaining world peace."

"Is Germany preparing for war?" asked Buddy Ebsen.

"Terms of the Versailles Treaty, signed after the Great War, won't allow it," replied Chamberlain. "Germany cannot re-arm, under its provisions. They can only maintain a small force for internal security."

"We've heard contrary rumors," said W.C. Fields.

"German émigrés have been showing up in Hollywood by the dozens," said Buddy Ebsen.

"Gravitating to the brighter lights, no doubt," replied Chamberlain. "Hollywood has become the pinnacle for entertainment."

"The rumors are more serious," replied Buddy Ebsen. "Jane has a letter from ..."

"Within Germany, the Bolsheviks and Jews have been outspoken with some grievances, I'll grant you," said Chamberlain, "regardless of their respective merits; but my military people tell me it appears to be focused internally. Hitler is a politician, and a very smart one at that. He was elected Chancellor by popular vote. Neighboring France, alone, has three times the standing army that Germany is allowed by the Versailles Treaty. Czechoslovakia, even, has more armed divisions. Hitler knows there'd be repercussions if he broke those terms... a fool's errand, no doubt."

"Can you inquire about Klaus Leonhardt?" asked Jane.

"I've read about him," replied Chamberlain. "Good actor. A German, too. My Embassy in Berlin keeps track of British citizens. It may be untoward to inquire about a German citizen, one of their own. But, to assure you, Miss Palmer, it's nothing that cannot be worked out in good time with diplomacy and patience. Take my word for it."

* * *

Jane wanted to visit Kenny's workplace while she was in London, but during her frequent phone calls, he'd begged off by inventing, 'other commitments'. She'd even volunteered to drive to Cambridge or Oxford, where she believed he was employed. Kenny couldn't invite her to the spy agency in the Broadway Buildings. That was out of the question.

The day following her final performance, a limousine delivered Jane to Teddington Memorial Hospital. She lunched with Teddy and available staffers, then toured the wards with Dr. Flemmer. Teddy returned to surgery.

"Jane Palmer is visiting us from Hollywood," said the doctor in each ward. "Teddy Kroneldt, one of our surgical nurses, is married to her brother."

Jane sang verses from *Aladdin*. Some patients knew the lyrics. She signed autographs, asked about their families. Late in the afternoon she strolled home with Teddy. Passersby stared.

"Kenny is always engrossed with his projects," said Teddy. "He never brings his work home," said Teddy. "Just a note pad. He stares into outer space with the blankest look... writes down cryptic numbers and symbols... talks in his sleep...mumbles strange words... like *stecker, rotor-settings, Turing machine, reciprocals*... wakes up in the middle of the night... doesn't come back to bed for an hour or two. He doesn't know he wakes me up. For God's sakes, Jane, don't ask him about his work. All you get is mumbo-jumbo. He loves it. I love him dearly."

An hour after they reached the house, Kenny arrived on his motorcycle, and took Jane for a ride. At a stop beside the Thames River, she related her meeting with the Prime Minister, and let him read the *Alfred Hugenberg* letter.

"I had planned to show it to Mr. Chamberlain," she said, "but, his reasoning about the situation in Germany made it seem inappropriate... impossible, in fact. After all, I was an guest in his home."

"I wish you had," replied Kenny.

"I wish you worked for some sort of spy agency, so you could help me find Klaus."

Chapter Thirteen

In February, 1938, Adolf Hitler abolished the entire War Ministry, replacing it with the new High Command of the Armed Forces (*Oberkommando der Wehrmacht or OKW*), headed by himself. It gave him day-to-day operations control of the Army, Navy, and Air Force. He bestowed upon himself a new title—*Der Fuehrer*. German newspapers characterized the changes as "a minor reorganization of the Home Guard to satisfy the current administration." British and American news outlets followed suit.

In a letter to Jane, Adrian Fisher penned: "Hitler may be striving to become king, possibly emperor, of an Aryan-dominated world. He's Caesar—in his mind."

Work at GC&CS exceeded capacity. Intercepts from Germany had increased 100-fold. Twelve cryptanalysts, along with dozens more clerks, were added to the staff. Four mathematicians were recruited by Alastair Denniston from Oxford and Cambridge to assist Turing and Kroneldt.

All of their work had been accomplished by hand. They'd developed punch cards, over which hand-perforated sheets—containing code-groups from recent intercepts—were carefully overlaid on a glass table. Lights, mounted underneath, illuminated any cipher match through the perforations. Though time-consuming, the system reduced the mind-boggling possibilities of rotor-settings down to a handful. A memo to Denniston detailed their success.

From 100 intercepts, about 12 will contain a repeated letter in the enciphered indicator. 12 repeats allow the sheets to eliminate all but 4 possible rotor-settings for each of the 6 possible Enigma wheel orders (123 132 213 231 312 321), leaving only 24 (6x4) possibilities to be tested. Type in a bit of the enciphered message text into the Enigma replica at each of 24 settings and watch whether sense or gibberish emerges.

To automate the process more, they wired together three pairs of Enigma replica machines. An electric motor rotated the rotors of all six, simultaneously, through the 17,576 possible positions of alphabetical settings (26 x 26 x 26). All rotors stopped when they hit a match. The cipher was recorded, and the electric motor was re-started, until the rotors hit a second match, then again for the third.

If the number of intercepts per day reached a fever pitch, and if the Germans changed the rotor-settings more frequently, GC&CS would never keep up by utilizing the time-consuming, manual system. Turing and Kroneldt designed specifications for an electro-mechanical machine—with high-speed cipher manipulation and repetition-detection capability—to replace the lengthy, luck-dependent, and human error-prone, perforated sheets and table-of-lights procedure.

Everyone at GC&CS was fearful that time was working against them.

* * *

The balcony in Parliament's House of Commons Chamber was packed with tourists.

Kenny, Alan Turing, 'C', and Alastair Denniston occupied reserved, front row seats overlooking the afternoon session. It was Kenny's first visit. He'd been invited to accompany them, and two others from the Foreign Office, for the anticipated purchase of Bletchley Park.

An unrelated, legislative matter had already been alternately blistered, satirized, commended, praised, and scolded by various Members of Parliament (MP's). Kenny was enthralled by the raucous banter and debate.

No one from the Foreign Office claimed to know what to expect from the Prime Minister. Information about the proposed acquisition had been "hush-hush", shielded from the press, even other government ministries. Neville Chamberlain's prior support of Intelligence funding was spotty.

Kenny remembered Jane's description of him—"tall and imperious… with a mustache and matching eyebrows… pitch descends when he talks slower… looks down his nose at you… could play a butler in a motion picture."

The Prime Minister began, without mincing words.

"I speak out against this proposed acqui-sition, all due respect to the sponsoring

minister. I pose a question, not only to the gentleman who brought this forward, but to all the Ministers who sit in this assembly, now and in the foreseeable future, in the following context: FUNDS ARE DEAR TO COME BY.

"God knows, we're all cognizant of that, without qualification. Our national treasury has, out of economic necessity, restraints, limits, priorities. We are in the grips of an economic blight that not only consumes all of Europe, but America, Asia, Australia, the world. I thank Almighty God that we, at the very least, enjoy world peace.

"With your forbearance, I shall precede my question by sharing with you this Sunday past. My wife and I drove our motorcar through the countryside on A-5 toward Bletchley, in Buckinghamshire. Such a beautiful day it was. Truly a portrait of England in full glow. We stopped along the way at a quaint inn beside the river, partook of a delightful, leisurely lunch, brown bread, green salad, baked beans, a grand assortment of poultry, fish, roast beef, pint of ale, anticipated with great expectation our first glimpse of the proposed property less than a half hour later that is described

on the public bill before you as 'ready for occupancy.'

What we discovered, to our disbelief , no, our utter astonishment! was not a gilded manor fit for a knight of the realm and his lady-in-waiting, as described in the narrative, but rather something out of Charles Dickens' Nicholas Nickleby *or* Oliver Twist, *take your pick. Some would call it an abomination. Others would more kindly refer to the facility as an architect's bad dream.*

"The fifty-five acre estate herein named Bletchley Park could very well be worth the price of 7500 pounds without *the existing real property standing on it, but rather with a new suitable structure in its place.*

"Charles Dickens' orphanage, as I think of it, deserves demolition, not habitation. What cost would then be asked of Parliament for its replacement or total rehabilitation if we acquiesce?

"Here is the question I put to you. With suitable, vacant buildings here in London, cannot you or any Minister find suitable, additional, facilities within manageable distance? 70 kilometers, that is the distance

from Whitehall to Bletchley Park, 70 kilometers I tell you.

"*Moreover, cannot you make do with your current accommodations during these economically trying times? It's difficult enough, at present, to locate you and your brethren. More so if we acquiesce? You will most certainly exceed arm's length. I implore you, sir, withdraw your petition.*

"*I understand your desire to host visiting dignitaries, to avail yourself of a getaway for planning, seminars, training, even a hunting preserve, or a retreat for vacationing staffers and their families, possibly even MP's. But now? Why now? What is the urgency?*

"*The biggest challenge facing the British Isles, the world at large, is the economic Depression. That, gentlemen, is the dragon we need to slay. No other!*

"*Our mandate is to avoid, at all costs, spending precious, limited resources for anything that is not totally committed to accomplishing that task, and assuring our constituent's well-being, safety, and opportunity to attain prosperity and the good life for future generations.*

"Take a deep breath. Make do. Now is not the time. Bletchley Park, in its present form, is not the place. Financial vigilance, gentlemen, and maintaining world peace that we've enjoyed since the Armistice in 1918, and expect to continue, will lead to Great Britain's and the world's economic recovery. Need I say more?

"'Nay', I pray, will be your appropriate response."

* * *

Walking beside Alan Turing, and close behind the Director and Denniston, on their somber return to the Foreign Office and Broadway Buildings, Kenny overheard 'C'.

"This won't stop us, Denniston,.." he said. "I'll purchase that bloody estate myself. There's nothing Mr. Chamberlain can do about *that*."

* * *

Consternation and frustration were daily emotions at GC&CS by late summer, 1938. Information from decryptions wasn't being heeded by Britain's politicians and military. If anything, it was ignored. Kenny attended frequent meetings discussing methods, not only how to speed up decryptions, but to incite action from Whitehall and uniformed services.

A visiting Royal Navy admiral lectured them, in a churlish tone, about the necessity to "read the tea leaves with skepticism...

leave their possible usefulness up to military experts... much of what you de-code is rubbish... you need only pass it along, not make judgments."

A recent glut of intercepts, originating from a plethora of German commanders, cited *Jack and Jill,* the children's nursery rhyme. It was a startling change of content. One interpretation speculated that *'Jack'* was Adolf Hitler; *Jill* —his trusted insider of high rank; the *'hill'*—Hitler's headquarters or scheduled destination; and *'fell down and broke his crown'*—the go-ahead to kill Hitler.

For what reason? How? If not Hitler, then who?

Some reasoned that *'Jack'* was the political leader of a border country—Austria, Czechoslovakia, or Poland. Others surmised a subterfuge—that *'Jack'*, wearing the uniform of a neighboring country, would appear to lead a force (*'Jill'*) from that country into a German border town (*'hill'*), cause a phony clash with civilians and militia (*pail of water*), get pursued back across the border (*'fell down and broke his crown'*); and thus create a propaganda victory that Hitler would use to justify invading that border country.

Such was the definition of a *phony war.*

Kenny recalled Jane's impassioned summary of *Lebensraum,* along with her account of Marlene Dietrich's mocking diatribe.

Another large group of decrypts, received within minutes of each other, lent credibility to the attempted *coup d'etat* theory. They referenced Shakespeare's drama, *Julius Caesar,* and Caesar's dying words to Brutus, who represented the alleged cabal, plotting Hitler's death.

"Who else could *Julius Caesar* possibly be?" asked the Watch Commander at GC&CS, in his memo to Alastair Denniston.

The London Daily Telegraph, on September 15, 1938, reported that Prime Minister Neville Chamberlain had flown to Berlin that morning to meet with Adolf Hitler, who'd invited him to discuss asking Czechoslovakia to cede the Sudetenland—its Western Region that abutted Germany's eastern border. Hitler promised he'd join England and France in guaranteeing the remainder of Czechoslovakia from any further aggression.

A diplomatic-coded message, intercepted at GC&CS later in the day, indicated that Chamberlain promised to take the proposition to Parliament. He'd asked Hitler to delay any plans for a military intervention.

Two days later, Chamberlain attained the approval from the House of Commons and the French government to acquiesce, and thus avoid war. Banner headlines heralded Chamberlain's *achievement.*

Kenny felt he was backstage at a theater, watching a live performance, as dozens of praiseful, coded messages flowed between European embassies. Conversely, GC&CS lamented the import and awful significance of the event. Disbelief reigned.

Hitler broadened his deception. He invited Poland and Hungary to get a piece of Czechoslovakia, in exchange for their cooperation. Agreement followed immediately.

Kenny watched Denniston kick a wastebasket against the wall, storm into his office, and slam the door shut.

Alan Turing whispered to Kenny, "Neville Chamberlain has his own peace agenda. He naively negotiates with a despot to prevent another war in Europe. The role of Intelligence will be elevated greatly …not shunted aside by the politicians and military, from this day forward."

On September 19, intercepts indicated that British and French Ambassadors in Prague adamantly urged the Czechs to relinquish Sudetenland, to preserve the peace— emphasizing that half the population were Germans.

Four days later, the *London Times* reported that Neville Chamberlain had re-visited Germany. Hitler informed him, in no uncertain terms, that the arrangement for Sudentenland would no longer suffice.

Der Fuhrer's motives were becoming apparent, as he changed the rules.

"I remain optimistic," said the Prime Minister, "that peace can still be maintained. Diplomacy is a powerful force. It's at work on all fronts."

GC&CS intercepts revealed a massing of German forces and equipment along the Czechoslovakian border. The Czechs countered, France mobilized, Britain put its fleet on alert and declared a state of emergency. For several consecutive nights Kenny did not motorcycle home to Teddington. He slept on a cot in the Broadway Buildings.

Neville Chamberlain attended a Joint Conference in Munich that included Adolf Hitler, Benito Mussolini from Italy, and Edouard Daladier—France's prime minister ten days later. Several representative from Czechoslovakia showed up, but were barred from the Conference Room. and awaited the decision in the hallway. The four attending heads-of-state signed the *Munich Agreement*—the political document that allowed the German army to occupy Sudentenland. Chamberlain praised the pact as, "the prelude to a permanent peace."

Winston Churchill stood up angrily in the House of Lords and roared, "... a total, unmitigated defeat!"

The following day, a GC&CS intercept read, "Jack's hill unclimbed. Fetch no water." Separately, various German commanders acknowledged acceptance.

"The coup is cancelled," Alan Turing told Kenny. "Europe lost."

John R. Downes

Early in the morning of October 1, German tanks and SS troopers invaded Sudentenland with unrelenting force and menace. A torrent of intercepts described panic and terror of the fleeing Czechoslovakians.

Chapter Fourteen

Jane stood alone at the edge of the red brick driveway that curled down onto Sunset Boulevard from the Moorish-style mansion on the Hollywood hillside. She admired the manicured lawn, foliage, and parade of towering palm trees that lined the perimeter. A gated entry and stucco wall fronted the estate.

Just before noon she'd signed the documents and remitted full payment to make the property her own. This was her first solo look at her new residence. Anonymity wouldn't last long. Passing motorists slowed down to gawk.

Months earlier, she'd parked out front with Klaus Leonhardt and imagined it as their home in wedlock. Practically every day since, she'd driven by, even stopped if traffic was light. Often, she cried. The real estate broker told her that the *'For Sale'* sign had been posted less than an hour before her query.

The Rogels and Fishers were supportive of her decision, but expressed concern about her living alone, even after she'd emphasized that the domestics she hired would occupy the servant's quarters; and out-of-town guests could remain as long as they wished. Already, the Fishers were planning a wintertime visit. She confided to Jack Wagner about providing housing for two un-married actresses or female studio employees, who "aren't party girls… until Klaus shows up."

Her decision to possess the coveted estate was torn between three motives—being constantly reminded of Klaus, *not* being constantly reminded of Klaus, *and* informing the world about their intention to marry. She chose to disclose the news to a *Los Angeles Times* reporter a week earlier. Two days later the story appeared in major newspapers throughout the United States. Magazine publicity followed. Telegrams deluged the studio from around the world praising the impending marriage. Some expressed relief regarding their faulty assumption that Klaus Leonhardt had reappeared.

Of course, he hadn't, but Jane reasoned that "spilling the beans"—contrary to her pact with Klaus—would pressure the Nazis to release him if they were, in fact, detaining him. She believed they were. At the very least, she hoped, they'd disclose his whereabouts. The glare of publicity caused heat.

*   *   *

Kenny was surprised to receive a letter at his Teddington residence that contained the return address of a U.S. Navy ship. It had been forwarded from the University of Nebraska in Lincoln to Dalton, Nebraska—then on to England. Six weeks had elapsed.

*

Dear Kenny;

Some friend I am—this being my first letter to you since graduation day. You probably thought I died. I haven't. As you can see on the envelope, I'm now Lieutenant j.g. (junior grade) Darrell Cassidy, Commanding Officer of the Navy Minesweeper, *USS Pochard ASR-22.* Home port is Norfolk, Virginia. Foreign port: Reykjavik, Iceland. Brrrr! Rotation every six months.

My own ship! Can you imagine?

My folks came by train from Santa Barbara for the Change-of-Command ceremony. Dad said the Fleet Admiral must like me. We've got a great crew!! He got to meet all of them—stayed on board for two hours.

Cornhuskers football practice is a picnic compared to OCS and Navy divers school. My scores were high at Officers Training, so I got to choose a specialty. Divers school it was. Six months of pure hell! But, I loved it. I'm suited for military life.

I expect you will become chairman of the mathematics department there eventually. What's 484 times 936? Quick! You would have made a fortune at OCS doing that trick. I told them about you. Nobody believed it.

The girls keep chasing me. Har-de-har-har! So
far I've eluded marriage. I'm waiting for the one
and only. A golden treasure like Teddy will do.

You two have something special.

Go, Cornhuskers!

Darrell
LT j.g. Darrell Cassidy

P.S. - Write when you can. Mail-call is a big daily
event in the Navy.

*   *   *

Kenny couldn't reveal his employer to Darrell—or anybody.
Simply ignoring the topic or not responding to his letter were un-
satisfactory options. He sought advice from Alastair Denniston,
who'd informed him that each person working for GC&CS, SIS,
and MI6 faced the same dilemma—including himself and 'C'.

*

Dear Darrell;

What a treat hearing from you and learning
about your recent promotion and important assignment. Need I find a way to salute by mail?
Teddy pinned your letter to the lampshade, and
together we bowed with due respect.

You will be surprised to find out I am on a paid sabbatical from *Nebraska* to develop mathematics programs and applications in association with Oxford and Cambridge wizards. Very very smart people. I stand in awe. Extremely difficult theorems to crack. Some we do. I feel like a small twig on a very large tree.

We live in Teddington, a small, quiet town in England, about half the size of Lincoln. It's a hop, skip and jump by train from London, en-route to both Oxford and Cambridge. There are lots of country roads for motorcycling with Teddy. She has the same job at Teddington Memorial Hospital as an operating room nurse that she had at Lincoln General. It's a short walk from our house.

My sister's star is shining. We got to see her 'live' in London last December. She played Aladdin! Hilarious. Packed the Palladium every night. Encores galore. Her motion pictures and records are very popular here.

Darrell—we know that the United States is safer knowing that you are in uniform. Thanks for serving. Thanks for being a good friend. Keep writing.

Anchors aweigh,
Kenny

Chapter Fifteen

The man from Poland looked fatigued and unkempt. He peered through loose-fitting bifocals at a thick document with 'C', Kenny, Alan Turing, and Alastair Denniston in the director's office. Twenty minutes earlier, Denniston had been summoned to appear with the two mathematicians.

M. Rejewski had arrived early in the morning at MI6, escorted by Polish Ambassador Edward Raczynski, to discuss a top-secret Intelligence matter. He'd flown all night from Warsaw in a civilian aircraft, skirting around Germany on the North, and refueling in Norway. He'd spent an hour briefing 'C' about his mission before the others arrived.

"Poland is gravely concerned about Germany's intentions," said 'C'. "Their operatives in Germany have forwarded to Warsaw foreboding reports in recent weeks. They mirror our own intercepts. Following Czechoslovakia's experience, the Polish government believes they're next on Hitler's menu. That's why Ambassador Raczynski and Mr. Rejewski are with us today. We've shared some of our Intelligence before you arrived. They trusted us with the Enigma machine replica. Now they're bringing us the *Bombe*."

To the layman's eyes, the electro-mechanical drawings in the document might have been initiated by Martians, or, at the very least, Thomas Edison in his Menlo Park, New Jersey laboratory. To Kenny Kroneldt and Alan Turing, they presented clarity and genius. For almost thirty minutes the pair engaged Rejewski about arcane elements such as *reciprocal letters, multiword cables*, identifying *steckers*, closed loops, rotor settings, *plain and cipher text*, wheel order, stops, starting positions, volume, speed, and Enigma machine linkages.

"You presently loop Enigmas together?" asked Rejewski in a mildly surprised tone.

"Three pairs," replied Turing. "We've recently discovered that matching strings of plain and cipher text are characteristic of a geometrical relationship dependent on wheel order and starting position, regardless of steckering."

"Impressive insight," said Rejewski. "Brilliant, in fact."

"We've begun to feed back contradictions into the loops," said Kenny, "rather than rejecting them out of hand."

"Another brilliancy," said Rejewski. "The *Bombe* will accommodate that by re-starting after a stop, without changing the wheel setting."

"What's your estimate to produce?" asked Denniston.

"How long does it take to build a Rolls-Royce?" asked the Ambassador. He smiled.

"I built the *Bombe* from scratch in sixty days with many tubes and panels from the telephone company," replied Rejewski. "Here in England?" He shrugged. "Your guess is as good as mine."

"They're handing the project over to us," said 'C'.

"Most respectfully ... for an expedited schedule," said the Ambassador.

"Rest assured," replied 'C'

"Mr. Rejewski will remain here to assist for whatever amount of time is necessary," said the Ambassador. "He'll be staying at the Embassy."

"Much to do," said 'C'. "So little time."

*   *   *

By the end of the week Alan Turing and Kenny were working with electrical engineers at the British Tabulating Company in Letchworth, twenty-four miles West of Cambridge. Their vision and task requirements for the finished product would be encompassed with Rejewsky's initial work on the *Bombe* machine, but with countless modifications from the assembled engineering/ mathematician team that would facilitate very high-speed, fast-changing applications, that could be operated by staffers, even clerks.

At the same time, Alastair Denniston had begun displaying on the conference room walls, newspaper articles about Nazi-caused events, that GC&CS had deciphered prior to publication.

March 13 - **SLOVAKIA & HITLER HOLD SUMMIT**
March 14 - **SLOVAKIA BREAKS FROM
               CZECHOSLOVAKIA**
March 15 - **CZECHOSLOVAKIA ASSEMBLY RELENTS**
March 16 - **CZECH LEFTOVERS - BOHEMIA &
               MORAVIA**
March 17 - **CHAMBERLAIN DISAVOWS CZECH
               PROTECTION**

March 18 - **CZECH PRESIDENT HACHA & HITLER TALK**

March 19 - **NAZIS REPUDIATE MUNICH AGREEMENT**

March 20 - **FRANCE PROTESTS GERMAN OCCUPATION**

March 30 - **CHAMBERLAIN PROMISES POLAND PROTECTION**

March 31 - **PARLIAMENT QUESTIONS APPEASEMENT POLICY**

April 1   - **STALIN REMAINS UNCOMMITTED**

* * *

Although the move by GC&CS, SIS, and MI6 to Bletchley Park from the Broadway Buildings and the Foreign Office had gone smoothly, local residents in Buckinghamshire and Bedfordshire didn't think so. Not knowing what was going on caused gossip and speculative news reports.

'C' invented story after story to allay fears and divert attention from its true purpose. He'd informed a *London Daily Telegraph* columnist that the property was designated to become a "research center for general aviation experiments."

The citizenry did not digest that well after the local newspaper editorialized that "Bletchley Park is not suited for a landing strip, or even hangars, for that matter. Cambridge or Oxford would make more sense."

Two of the more credible rumors whispered that the telephone utility was relocating equipment and employees from London to the site; the other being a post office mail-sorting facility—"away from the hustle and bustle of the metropolis."

When workmen were seen installing underground telephone cables between the mansion and the post office, then a new water main from the nearby reservoir, and finally, a new approach road—completely paved—from the highway, citizen unrest was replaced by reluctant acceptance for whatever purpose that resulted.

Since May, when news leaked about the mysterious new owner of Bletchley Park, government vehicles and busses were seen queued up in the driveway, and parked at inns and lodging places in Milton-Keynes, Fennie Stratford, Bedford, Aylesbury, and other nearby towns. Tourists couldn't book a room. Ale houses thrived. Newcomers were queried by locals about the "goings-on at the mansion", while playing darts and shuffleboard in the drinking establishments, shopping at the bakery, or stopped at an intersection. The standard replies became, "… a storage facility and library for government papers," and, "… involved in research, archives, and cataloguing."

Kenny was one of a handful of insiders who knew that 'C' was the purchaser. The press had only been told it was British government property.

The new location gave the mathematicians room and privacy they didn't have on the third floor of the Broadway Buildings.

In the mix of existing structures at Bletchley Park, a cottage—adjacent to the mansion—provided adequate work space for the mathematicians, and living quarters for one person or married couple. Alan Turing moved in solo. The four new mathematicians opted for hotels and inns in nearby towns, along with about one hundred other employees, all scrambling for living quarters at once. Kenny planned to commute thirty kilometers every day from Teddington.

The mansion housed the Naval, Army, and Air sections of GC&CS on the ground floor—along with the telephone exchange, tele-printer room, kitchen, and banquet-sized dining room. MI6 and SIS took over the second floor. The mansion's water tower became the wireless room. Militarily, the facility was designated Station X—Great Britain's tenth listening post worldwide.

The mansion was jam-packed with an assortment of spies, academics, cryptanalysts, telegraphers, clerks, and assistants. Preparation and organization had begun in earnest for the inevitable war.

Separate *Huts* were in the planning stages, or already under construction, for separate Intelligence and decryption operations of each service branch and activity—Navy, Air, Army, diplomatic, hand ciphers, telegraphy—even a brick building for the *Bombe* machine, and its soon-to-be-built replicas.

Chapter Sixteen

Knowing a devastating event was imminent seemed almost as fearsome as the event itself; waiting for the moment of its occurrence caused dread and foreboding.

That's how Kenny felt about some decryptions. Taking action on the information wasn't the role for code-breakers or Intelligence—only decryption, interpretation, and dissemination. GC&CS and SIS were the first to learn about Hitler's plans, and although the British military and government officials were apprised through proper channels, the most recent decrypts required *action* from the House of Commons, under the leadership of Prime Minister Neville Chamberlain. That's how British democracy worked.

By mid-August the *Bombe* was operational, subject to myriad daily adjustments, experiments, and guidance from Rejewsky. The 3-cipher Enigma machine rotor settings, with the application of appropriate *cribs* and educated guesses, were being determined hours faster than before. However, the volume of coded messages had increased immeasurably—hundreds more per day—between the Nazi High Command and military Divisions that were massing up along the German-Polish border.

Hitler summoned his generals to Berchtesgaden for a conference. Newspapers reported that Germany and Russia had just signed a Non-Aggression Pact, leaving him free of worry about fighting a war on two fronts. Alastair Denniston recruited talent much of the time. Neville Chamberlain advocated that peace was still at hand—in countless interviews and addresses to Parliament.

* * *

Jane tore open the envelope postmarked Berlin.

She'd just driven home from an exhausting day of filming at Wagner Studios, spotted the letter in the clutter of mail, and slumped down against the wall of her foyer to read it.

Adlon Hotel, Berlin

Dear Miss Palmer,

Adrian Fisher asked me to write to you. He gave me your address. Out of respect for your privacy, I will not share it with anyone.

I have striven every which way I can to learn the whereabouts of Klaus Leonhardt. My wife told me she believed it would be easy. It has not been.

High-ranking military and government officials are guests in my hotel. My discreet inquiries have accomplished nothing other than shrugs, disdainful looks, or rebukes. I am at a complete loss as to the reasons why? He is a very popular figure and recognized by everybody.

You will receive this letter only because an imbibing, friendly, army colonel staying here has agreed to post it for me tomorrow when he departs to join his unit.

The military has been put on alert. For several weeks now there have been reports in the press and remarks by several hotel guests about organized pillaging up North in some of our border towns by Polish renegades. They need to stay where they belong. God help them if they come to Berlin!

Klaus Leonhardt's film, Lebesraum, *has been showing constantly since before the Olympics. Déjà vu!*

My wife and I believe that he will show up. We surmise he is filming a picture in a secret location, not wanting to be bothered by reporters and such. He is too well-known and liked for somebody not to locate his whereabouts somewhere, someplace, somehow. We feel positive about that, as does your own father— God bless him. Adrian has been a beacon of light and role-model for me over the years with his hotel prowess.

*I will keep you informed about Klaus Leonhardt
as I learn things. You may count on me. Anytime!
Ask and it shall be done.*

*Poland is causing a clampdown and tight secu-
rity by the military throughout Germany that I do
not expect to last very long. Unfortunately, Polish
leaders in Warsaw appear to be following Czechoslovakia's lead, fools that they are.*

*Letters you address to me will get through in due
course. The postal union strike is settled.*

Respectfully,

Louis Lorenz

* * *

September 1, 1939

Kenny stared at the decrypt on the bulletin board.

'C' had pinned it there himself before he strode through the
various offices of the mansion, then out to the cottage and various
Huts, demanding that everyone read it. He then jumped into his
Lancia convertible and sped away, with tires screeching.

Mrs. Pemberton whispered that he was "off to London to
meet with Prime Minister Chamberlain, Foreign Secretary Hali-
fax, and others. I've never seen him in such a lather."

The work protocol at GC&CS and SIS separated tasks completely—not just between cryptanalysts and spies, but within each

of the two specifically-tasked agencies. The radio operators listened for and wrote down the coded messages, then turned them over to the mathematicians and *Bombe* operators, who needed to determine the Enigma machine's rotor-setting for that day or week.

Alan Turing and Kenny reminded staffers at every meeting that they required a minimum of eighty intercepts—plus the available *cribs*—before commencing their task, to keep the odds for success in their favor. That was usually accomplished early in the day. But not always. Some days, not at all.

Then it was the cryptanalysts turn. They converted the coded messages into plain text, using a replica of the Enigma machine with the rotors properly set.

The decrypts were forwarded to the Watch Commander. He determined whether they were important enough to send on—first to 'C', then to a military command or embassy or the Prime Minister or government agency or any number of other possible recipients.

It had been commonplace for newspaper headlines to be posted on the bulletin board, but never a decrypt until that day. It's one that Adolf Hitler sent to his General Staff and all Field Marshals.

*

"I shall give the propagandists reasons for war. Never mind whether starting a war is plausible or not. The victor will not be asked afterward whether he told the truth or not. In starting and waging a war it is not right that matters, but victory. Close your hearts

to pity. Act brutally. Eighty million people must obtain what is their right. The stronger man is right. Be harsh and remorseless. Be steeled against all signs of compassion. Believe, Obey, Fight!"

/s/ Adolf Hitler, Der Fuehrer - Oberkommando der Wehrmacht

*

Dozens of ensuing messages from Polish Army units along the German-Poland border were decrypted rapidly, and forwarded to 'C' for his meetings in London.

*

Fake raids by Polish Army underway. Emphasize fake. Prisoners from German concentration camps riddled with bullets— dressed in Polish uniforms— posed to look like they were killed while invading Germany.

*

Gliewitz Poland radio station captured by Germans. Broadcasting in Polish. Pretending to be Polish. Begging Poles to attack. German ruse. Our attempts to knock station off the air— so far— have not succeeded.

*

*Dozens of German armored divisions cross-
ing border at will in multiple positions.
Crushing our resistance. Slaughter occurring. Hundreds dead. Vicious assault. Un-
stoppable. No retreat is requested. Need assistance.*

*

German newspapers reported Adolf Hitler's description of the
invasion in a speech before the Reichstag in Berlin later that day.

*"Last night for the first time, Polish soldiers
fired on our own territory. Since 5:45 a.m.
we have been returning the fire. From now
on, bombs will be met with bombs."*

*

The next day Prime Minister Neville Chamberlain addressed
Parliament. "Adolf Hitler is the commonest little swine I have
ever encountered."

Chapter Seventeen

England went dark.

A city-wide silence awaited a German attack. Windows were covered, emergency power generators readied, gas masks distributed, air raid sirens tested, school evacuation drills begun, bomb shelters prepared. Winston Churchill returned to his position as First Lord of the Admiralty. British and French military forces adopted a defensive posture. Ambassadors from many nations talked. And talked. And talked.

The fearful public waited.

* * *

Dr. Flemmer at Teddington Memorial Hospital briefed the nursing staff—one-at-a-time. It was Teddy's turn.

"We need to anticipate war," he said. "You may go home to America if you like. If you choose to remain in England, you will be assigned to a military field unit. You will have no choice in the matter. Surgical nurses are essential in wartime. You will carry the temporary rank and pay grade of Royal Army Major."

"When?"

"No one has a crystal ball."

* * *

Bletchley Park's task had grown exponentially more challenging. Kenny, Alan Turing, and the other mathematicians realized that the German's had re-configured the Enigma machines.

A staffer pinned a note on the bulletin board. "We're going to get you good, Hitler." Dozens initialed it.

For several weeks following the invasion of Poland, intercepts translated into gobbledygook. That could only mean the Germans had added a rotor, perhaps two.

Kenny calculated that the number of possible 3-cipher settings had increased from the previous 17,576 to 456,976—if four rotors (26 x 26 x 26 x 26); and to 11,881,37—if five rotors (26 x 26 x 26 x 26 x 26). Even with ample *cribs* and extraordinary guesswork to reduce the possibilities, the remaining number to cope with would be staggeringly huge.

"Theoretically, the *Bombe* machine can deal with it," said Turing, "given enough time."

But instead of an hour or two, the additional rotors could mean a week or more of running time on the *Bombe*, before it hit the magic combination of ciphers—if at all.

Further complicating their task was the agreed-upon assumption that each German military branch utilized different code settings—even different Enigma machine rotor configurations. More problematic was that German army and Luftwaffe units frequently used the same telegraphy network. Separating those messages became one more cobweb for Bletchley Park to unravel.

Navy (Kriegsmarine) ciphers had become inscrutable. Recent intercepts could not be deciphered. 'C' coined the word, *floradora*, in a memo acknowledging the "maze of difficulty". He mandated they be "top priority" for Turing and Kroneldt.

* * *

Three weeks later

"German ships are headed for the Norwegian coast," said Kenny. He stood with Alan Turing and the Watch Commander just inside 'C's office on the mansion's second floor.

"Lazy German telegraphers have provided us with a break-through," said Turing, standing beside Kenny. "It's not *Floradora*. They're utilizing the 3-rotor Enigmas. Worse for them … with last week's code settings."

"Norway's Ambassador is emphatic that his country is next in Hitler's grab bag," replied 'C'. "My field agents concur, but the Admiralty considers it speculative. They say it would spread German forces too thin. England's a target. Hitler is preoccupied with Czechoslovakia and Poland."

"The latest intercepts," said the Watch Commander, "ordered ships headed for Bergen, Norway to report their positions to the War Office in Berlin."

"Ha ha ha. What a way to run a war," replied 'C'. "Any Navy man knows you don't do that. Army is controlling this operation. Menace of Hitler, the loopy megalomaniac… he tipped us off. They're troopships, all right. I'll let the Admiralty know. Have a seat. I want the three of you to bring me up-to-date on *Floradora*."

Within two minutes he was characterizing the intercepts on a direct, scrambled, telephone line.

"Just minutes ago," he replied to a question, after he'd completed his narrative. His face turned red. "I know that ships report to Naval headquarters, but these are not. That's how we know they're troopships… they're troopships… this is Army, not Navy … no… Bletchley Park is not a bunch of egghead professors presuming to tell you how navies operate… my crew doesn't need to know Navy customs, they need only read the intercepts… may I remind you, I'm Navy… my God, man, don't you realize that this signals an invasion of Norway? What else could it mean?… you're waiting for corroboration?… how about Poland, Czechoslovakia, my own agents on the ground, Norway's Ambassador, now these intercepts? How about a death count?"

*   *   *

Kenny shared C's frustration. He'd heard him vent to his superiors on numerous occasions. Coping with resistance and skepticism was no fun. Brick wall might be a better characterization. He knew the truth—they didn't.

Those outbursts reminded Kenny of University President Auerbach's disparagement of American Intelligence, while he was espousing Britain's superiority.

> *"We have no version. Only inter-service rivalries, distance from the Great War battlefields, a peacetime mentality, old-school military philosophies, a resistance to change, and most recently, a profound ignorance of reality."*

Perhaps there was no difference.

One of 'C's oft-repeated expressions, "Like pulling elephants through hardening rubber," had unambiguous reference to many of his military and political brethren and their barely-disguised distrust of intelligence-gathering—even after detected German atrocities occurred.

Ruses, exaggerations, faulty interpretations, tactical deceit, error-strewn, uncorroborated, were a few of their rationalizations for denials.

On the one hand, MI6, SIS, and GC&CS knew from decrypts and secret agents that war had been in the making for months—years; on the other, the political leadership expressed *hope,* and promoted the myth of negotiated peace, while disdaining and downplaying accumulated evidence that indicated the contrary. Constant diplomacy and believing the bad guys were at the top of their agenda. After all, it had been twenty-one years since the Armistice in 1918 that ended the "war to end all wars." Peace-advocates cited the Versailles Treaty over and over, ad nauseum, as a crutch to support their assertion that the Germans couldn't re-arm, even if they wanted to. A treaty prevented that, they said.

*   *   *

Kenny flipped pancakes and served breakfast while Teddy read aloud the front page story in the newspaper. It was one of their rare days-off together. They'd planned a motorcycle ride along the Thames river for a picnic, but drizzly weather caused them to stay home.

The headline read: *GERMANY INVADES NORWAY.*

"Why couldn't someone on our side have found out about this before it happened?" asked Teddy.

"I'm sure military and government people are asking themselves the same question," replied Kenny.

"Adolf Hitler can't be that smart, can he?"

"He was a corporal in the Austrian army."

Ha ha ha, that's good. Pass the syrup. Listen to this quote from Winston Churchill."

> *"In the face of a vastly superior British fleet,*
> *the Germans landed troops up and down*
> *the coast of Norway with surprise, ruthless-*
> *ness, and precision in the predawn hours...*
> *an avoidable outrage allowed by idealism,*
> *naiveté, and dearth of vigilance."*

"Let's hope Neville Chamberlain's days are numbered," said Kenny.

"When?" asked Teddy.

"No one listens to us academic types."

Chapter Eighteen

On May 10, 1940, two major war events occurred. The Nazis invaded Holland and Belgium; and Winston Churchill replaced Neville Chamberlain.

"My warnings over the last six years," proclaimed the new Prime Minister during his swearing-in ceremony, "have been so numerous, so detailed, and have been so terribly vindicated, that no one can gainsay me."

Cheers went up throughout Bletchley Park.

* * *

The upsurge in German intercepts, following the invasion of Poland, caused Kenny to study the pattern of signals—where they came from, who they were transmitted to, and how much traffic was carried at different times of day. He believed that just those factors by themselves might make it possible to deduce movement of troops, ships, and supplies, the order of battle—even if the intercepts could not be read. He briefed Denniston by referring to his study as, *Traffic Analysis*.

Shortly thereafter, he noticed a spike in German intercepts from the Northwest coast of Norway, directly West of Narvik. He reported it to Alastair Denniston, who called for an immediate meeting with 'C' and the Watch Commander.

Kenny was prepared. He produced a chart showing the intercepts by sender, receiver, and time of day. Within the previous forty-eight hours, ninety-seven had been transmitted between three German cruisers—*Schornhorst, Gneisenau, Hipper*— and German Naval Headquarters.

"We've decrypted only a few, although we've sourced most of the rest," said the Watch Commander, following Kenny's presentation. "Normal stuff. Change of positions, acknowledgments, weather reports, banter between captains."

"Just what one would expect?" said 'C'. He stood and shook hands with Kenny.

"Good show, Kroneldt. Ingenious! Those Nazis are up to no good. Narvik is in their sights… during the evacuation, no less. Yours is the right call. You deserve a pat on the back. The Admiralty won't be able to drag their feet on this one. I'll dispatch your *Kroneldt Traffic Analysis* immediately."

* * *

Three days later, Kenny arrived for his early morning shift, and parked his motorcycle beside the cottage. Alan Turing ran out, took him by the arm, and led him into the mansion. "We just lost an aircraft carrier and two destroyers," said Turing. "All hell's breaking loose." Staffers were crowded in front of the bulletin board, reading posted decrypts.

"Is it Norway?" asked Kenny.

"Our carrier, *HMS Glorious*, was evacuating refugees from Narvik... ahead of the German army advance," replied Turing. "It left port yesterday with two destroyers. They've been sunk. More than fifteen-hundred missing, presumed drowned."

Kenny read the flurry of intercepts—the result of the Admiralty's inaction. He felt like a helpless brother of an ancient Roman gladiator.

0430 - GERMAN BATTLE CRUISER
    SCHARNHORST:
    CONFIRM SIGHTING OF ENEMY
    AIRCRAFT CARRIER.

0432 - GERMAN BATTLE CRUISER
    GNEISENAU:
    CONFIRM SIGHTING OF BRIT-
    ISH CARRIER ACCOMPANIED BY 2
    DESTROYERS.

0434 - GERMAN NAVAL COMMANDER,
    ADMIRAL RAEDER: ONLY 2 DE-
    STROYERS? RECONFIRM MSG.

0437 - GERMAN BATTLE CRUISER,
    GNEISENAU:
    REPEAT. 2 BRITISH DESTROYERS
    1 AIRCRAFT CARRIER IN SIGHT.
    CONFIRMED.

0441 - GERMAN HEAVY CRUISER, HIPPER:
SIGHTING RECONFIRMED. BRIT-
ISH AIRCRAFT CARRIER GLORI-
OUS ACCOMPANIED BY 2 DE-
STROYERS.

0445 - GERMAN NAVAL COMMANDER,
ADMIRAL RAEDER: LAUNCH
SIMUL ATTACK AT 0520.

0520 - GERMAN HEAVY CRUISER, HIPPER:
COORDINATED ATTACK UNDER-
WAY.

0526 - GERMAN BATTLE CRUISER,
SCHARNHORST:
DIRECT HIT ON CARRIER. MUL-
TIPLE FIRES AMIDSHIP. LEANING
TO PORT.

0532 - GERMAN HEAVY CRUISER, HIP-
PER:
BRITISH DESTROYER HIT AND
SINKING.

0543 - GERMAN BATTLE CRUISER,
SCHARNHORST:
MULTIPLE DIRECT HITS ON CAR-
RIER. BRIDGE DESTROYED.
SINKING RAPIDLY. ABANDON-
MENT UNDERWAY.

Kenny couldn't read more. Very slowly, he made his way to the wash room, and threw up in the toilet.

* * *

Kenny viewed Scapa Flow from the bridge of the battleship, *HMS Hood*. He stood with binoculars beside Chief Admiral Andrew Cunningham, who'd invited him for a fortnight-long, and unimpeded look, at Royal Navy communications, defensive and offensive tactics regarding ships and submarines, and signal identification procedures. His itinerary included two days and nights aboard each of three battleships and three destroyers

Denniston had informed Kenny the invitation was instigated by the infuriated Winston Churchill.

"Recent losses might very well have been avoidable by not ignoring our intelligence," said Denniston. "Every flag officer has read your *Kroneldt Traffic Analysis* by now. They covet exculpation."

Scapa Flow served as the chief Naval base and headquarters for the Admiralty. Located in Scotland, it was sheltered by the Orkney islands of Mainland, Graemsay, Burray, South Ronaldsay, and Hoy. Its reputation as one of the great natural harbors in the world dated back more than a thousand years as an anchorage for Viking ships.

Kenny had been wined and dined as though he were visiting royalty — with access to the Admiral's launch, any moored ship, and all shipboard departments. He spent most of his time with radar, radio, and hydrophone operators, and in the officers' wardrooms, where he attended meetings and made presentations.

"Obtaining Intelligence is a 4-pronged effort," he told each assemblage. "First... *receiving intercepts and transcribing* them exactly. All of you on the front lines and MI6 ... with listening posts all over the globe... share that task.

"Second... *decoding the intercepts.* That's one of the major tasks for MI6. Know that the enemy is constantly changing its code book and encrypting equipment to frustrate our efforts. MI6 has assembled some of the smartest people in the world to counter those changes.

"Third, *well-placed field agents,* whom you would refer to as spies. That, too, is a major task for MI6. Other nations partner with us in this endeavor. Their skill level is Sherlock Holmes to the tenth power... their bravery and wiliness is like that of Lawrence of Arabia.

"Fourth... *captured ships.* That is completely your bailiwick. When you approach and prepare to board one, remember, first and foremost, that the fleeing crew has standing orders to scuttle it.

"Before the ship or U-boat goes down, the treasure you seek, in priority order, is first ... *the code book.* It's an innocent-looking, loose-leaf notebook, or bound journal.

"Second... the *enciphering machine.* It contains a standard-looking typewriter keyboard. A sailor can lift it, but it is quite heavy. It's preferable to use two hands. The most important parts on the enciphering machine are the *rotors.* Some have three... some four... some may eventually have five. Rotors are easily removed by unclipping an accessible spring, then simply lifting them out... one-at-a-time. Captured crew members may be carrying them off their ship in their pockets ... planning to drop them into the sea ... forever lost. Rotors may be hidden in a sea bag they've tossed overboard. That's valuable debris. Don't ignore it."

No one, except the Admiral, heard the words, *Bletchley Park* or *enigma* mentioned—only MI6. *"Professor Kroneldt from British intelligence"*—as he was introduced—presented a boxful of recent

German decrypts and intercepts to illustrate the importance of error-free transcriptions by wireless operators—and the back-and-forth exchanges between Commanders leading up to a final result.

A hydrophone operator asked Kenny, "Any Yanks, besides you, coming to help us, Professor?"

"Many of my peers served during the Great War," said Admiral Cunningham, while alone with Kenny on the bridge. "Commissioned officers considered it ungentlemanly to peek at other people's mail... and heeded warnings only from the crow's nest. Times have changed. Like Pequod's Ahab, we found it necessary to see the white whale for ourselves."

Chapter Nineteen

DECEMBER 1940

Jane bowed in acknowledgment to the applause for her command performance in the crowded East Room of the White House. President Roosevelt smiled from his wheelchair in the front row. Eleanor sat beside him with Jane's adoptive parents.

Adrian Fisher had been invited to Washington, D.C. for a week-long economic conference that coincided with Jane's scheduled appearance. Jane and the Fishers had been asked to join the Roosevelts in their living quarters following the concert and reception.

"I invite your candid views, Adrian, regarding that damned war in Europe... and our ongoing economic Depression," said the President after pleasantries were exchanged, brandy poured, and Jane's singing talent lauded in a toast. "First, I wish to share a portion of a letter with you that I received from Winston Churchill." He unfolded and read it aloud.

"The decision for 1941 lies upon the seas. England has lost 400,000 tons of ship-

ping in one five-week period alone. At any point, Vichy France might surrender the French fleet to Hitler under duress, despite its promises to the contrary. That would tip the balance cataclysmically against the Royal Navy.

"My hope is that American merchant ships begin carrying war supplies to Britain, guarded by American warships. Britain has depleted its funds for what we desperately need.

"I believe you will agree that it would be wrong in principle and mutually disadvantageous in effect if at the height of this struggle Great Britain were to be divested of all sellable assets, so that after the victory was won with our blood, civilization saved, and the time gained for the United States to be fully armed against all eventualities, we should stand stripped to the bone."

Nobody spoke for a whole minute after President Roosevelt slowly refolded the letter and laid it aside.

"My response to the Prime Minister may be the most important of my presidency," he said. "You have the floor, Adrian."

Without hesitation, Adrian Fisher began. "One of my most loyal hotel guests is the chairman of a large manufacturer. He employs dozens of sales reps and utilizes numerous suppliers who travel the Midwest. Over the years his company has booked hundreds of rooms and food service for them for overnight and weeklong stays, sales meetings, and conventions in each of my hotels. They haven't been spared from hard times. He shares my optimism for the economic recovery. I let him know how much I appreciate his business and offered him a proposition. I would carry a tab for his continuing patronage and not be a cash drain on his limited revenue stream. When business gets back to normal, we can plan repayment. It represents a very small percentage of his expense structure, but it contributes."

"Who would turn that down?" asked Eleanor Roosevelt.

"No one with honest motives and good credit," replied Adrian.

"You've done that time after time, Father," said Jane.

"Altruism and pragmatism stirred together, Sweetheart," replied Adrian. "I'm a businessman. I have the facilities. Every hotel owner's daily question is, 'Occupancy or vacancy?' My vote is for the former… calculated risk for *something*, versus guaranteed assurance for *nothing*."

"Mr. President," said Jane, "Mr. Churchill asked if you would *carry war supplies to Britain*. Doesn't that mean putting our factories back to work?"

"Ha ha ha. Of course it does, Jane," he replied.

*   *   *

Two weeks later

Kenny was one of six patrons waiting his turn for a haircut in the Teddington barber shop. Excited conversations, led by both barbers, praised a single subject—the front page story in the Saturday morning edition of the *London Daily Telegraph*. The banner headline read:

LEND-LEASE AMERICA
COMES TO OUR RESCUE

Earlier in the week, Bletchley Park had already decrypted President Roosevelt's decision from Embassy intercepts, then passed them along to the Prime Minister, via 'C', who called an emergency meeting of the mathematicians and Naval cryptanalysts.

"Keeping up with *Kriegsmarine* intercepts has become imperative," he told them. "America will be counting on us to warn their merchant vessels and Navy escorts about U-boats lurking in the Atlantic. U.S. freighters, loaded with military armament, supplies, and food, will be headed for our shores. That's what Lend-Lease America means. President Roosevelt has called upon his Congress to *lend* our country whatever we need to defeat the Nazis. He's allowing Great Britain to pay for it, when this war ends and Hitler is dead. Praise God. Those freighters must navigate a route where the U-boats are not."

"This is a stroke of genius," exclaimed a waiting barber shop patron, as he perused the news story.

Everyone chimed in.

"Roosevelt claims that his sole purpose is to keep America out of the war."

"Political rationales come in all disguises."

"He said America must be the *arsenal of democracy*."

"America's been neutral up to now."

"Lend-lease is an un-neutral act, masquerading as neutrality."

"That's what makes it so stunningly brilliant."

"Professor Kroneldt from Oxford University is with us," said a barber. "He's an American. Let's hear what he has to say."

All turned to look at Kenny. He'd not participated in the discussion.

"I am very proud of my country," he said.

* * *

Dear Kenny,

Guess what? I just got engaged! Her name is Lola Watson. She lives in Newport News, Virginia with two roommates. They work together at the Navy Shipyard as civilian secretaries. I met her at an Officer's Club dance two months ago. We've been practically inseparable since.

Lola is from Lebanon, Tennessee, near Nashville. Her parents both work at the Texas Boot Company there. Practically everybody in town does. You should hear her Southern accent. She got everyone's attention during the Fleet picnic at the Naval Station.

I popped the question last week.

The *Pochard* just got orders to rotate to Iceland. Two months ahead of schedule! We're eloping. I don't want you sailing across the Pacific to attend our wedding. It's too dangerous. I will consider you my *best man* in absentia, old friend.

The Atlantic Fleet has been put on convoy duty for merchant ships and passenger liners. It's all part of Roosevelt's recently-announced Lend-Lease program. You probably haven't heard much about that. The U.S. Navy has!

The war is sweeping us up in its fury. I'm ready. My ship and crew are in fighting trim. We go out every day for operation exercises. I can't tell you what we do, but it's important.

Note my new mailing address below, even when I'm in Iceland. Brrr again.

Test question: Is the *Pochard* a minesweeper or an ice-cutter? Har-de-har-har.

Keep writing.

Go, Cornhuskers!

Darrell
LT j.g. Darrell Cassidy
USS Pochard ASR-22
APO 860
c/o Postmaster
New York, NY

*

To: Major Theodora (Teddy) Pawelsky Kroneldt

From: QAIMNS (Queen Alexandra's Imperial Military Nursing Service)

Subj: Commission to Matron (Major), Call to Duty

This letter confirms your EMERGENCY COMMISSION as Matron (equivalency of Army Major) in QAIMNS.

Report for 14 days Officer Indoctrination at 0800 on 18 March 1940 to QAIMNS HQ, War Office, London. Orders to duty station will follow.

Congratulations and welcome.

Your sister in service,

Dame Katharine Jones
Matron-in-Chief (Brigadier General)

Chapter Twenty

The winding road from Teddington to Buckingham was virtually free of traffic during the early morning hour. In recent months, the route had become Kenny's favorite for motorcycle rides—this time, though, without Teddy. It was the first leg of a circle trip that included Aylesbury, Stony Stratford, Oxford, with stops for breakfast and lunch, then back to Teddington.

The time spent was productive. Kenny daydreamed without interruption. Insights and solutions for Bletchley Park occurred frequently.

The present was a crucial time. German Navy intercepts had become unreadable since the Nazis invaded Norway. Pressure from the Admiralty was intense. 'C' received daily reminders from Winston Churchill regarding the importance of discovering the whereabouts of U-boats, to guarantee the success of U.S. merchant ship convoys crossing the Atlantic.

The mathematicians conjectured that the Nazis had re-wired each rotor on the Enigma machine differently, inter-changed rotors as often as every day, and allowed encrypters to randomly select four (maybe even five) from as many as eight different rotors.

The possible variations numbered 1 followed by 20 zeros, making 17,576—the previous number—minuscule in comparison.

If MI6 agents could obtain a Nazi code book—along with newly-re-wired rotors, the "table would be set" for building a new library of *cribs*, reduce the number of variations, and quickly lead to a consistent and rapid reading of future German Naval intercepts.

Kenny couldn't keep the challenge out of his mind."

> *What if the Royal Air Force captured an operable German bomber, manned it with a German-speaking RAF pilot and crew wearing German uniforms, then purposely crashed it into the English Channel, while sending out an SOS for a German rescue ship?*

Crisp March air buffeted Kenny's face. An occasional pedestrian waved with a friendly gesture. Familiar sights included creek-spanning bridges, a diversity of eating establishments and roadside inns, plus acres and acres of green, open spaces, bedecked with wildflowers heralding the approaching summer. English greens were richer than Nebraska's—the birds more colorful.

Peace and quiet belied the reality that a war was going on. Even though the whole of the British Isles had been put on alert for the past several months—awaiting an invasion by the Nazis—life was going on. Daily chores were accomplished, schools were in session, the countryside looked no different.

> *When the German rescue ship arrived at the scene, a British ship would commandeer it, capture the crew, then tow it to the nearest port.*

Each day of Teddy's absence seemed like a week. This time, he was the one who'd been left behind. Previously, she'd been the one—during his initial trip from Lincoln by himself, then recently, to Skapa Flow. She never complained, nor would he. What a difference, though, being the one who leaves compared to the one left behind.

At the very least, the former faced an adventure of some sort, whereas the latter—only loneliness.

It was possible that her unknown, future assignment would separate them for months at a time. They'd not been given a clue whether she'd remain in England. Army nurses served anywhere they were needed.

> *The Enigma machine with the re-wired rotors and code book would be removed from the German vessel, and rushed to Bletchley Park.*

Kenny steered onto a side road, turned around, and headed toward the highway leading to his workplace.

*   *   *

Three days after Kenny delivered his written plan in a sealed envelope to Mrs. Pemberton, 'C' summoned him to his office for a private chat.

"Admiral Cunningham asked me who came up with this 'hare-brained, ingenious plan'," said 'C'. "I simply answered, 'Kroneldt'. Ha ha ha. He respects you, Professor. He gave it the green light. I tinkered with it a little, but you deserve all the credit."

"Is the Admiral always that blunt?" asked Kenny.

"War requires it. Lives are always at risk. My own concern was the lack of a cover story. The Germans must not discern we seek a prize bigger than a rescue ship. Cunningham has already contacted the RAF for a suitable pilot and crew. The air ministry has the German bomber. operation-ready. It's hangared at Dover."

"May I inquire about the cover story?"

"Thrill seekers. Smilin' Jack and his crew... fresh out of flight school... yearn to blow the Nazis into oblivion, single-handedly... seeking glory. They steal the bomber, know they'll get in trouble, but believe that the resulting ship capture will mitigate any punishment... maybe even earn them a medal."

"Are cover stories always so convoluted?"

"Ha ha ha. You better know, Professor. You won't be able to deny you came up with this one."

They heard three knocks on the door. Kenny watched 'C' flip a toggle switch beside his desk. After a pause, Mrs. Pemberton peeked in.

"Dame Katharine Jones returned my call," she said.

"You may speak candidly," replied 'C'.

The gatekeeper stepped in and shut the door. "It's about your wife, Professor. I know where she's going."

"Tell us," said 'C'.

"Egypt... with the British Eighth Army Command. She's been designated to head up a Surgical Nursing Group."

"Major Kroneldt has a nice ring to it," said 'C'.

"When?" asked Kenny.

"First Monday in June," replied Mrs. Pemberton. "She, most likely, will have a portable address."

"German Field Marshal Erwin Rommel's reputation precedes him. His tanks are menacing African and port cities on the Mediterranean."

"Teddy and I agreed that anywhere she goes," said Kenny, "she'll be in close proximity to Hitler's Nazis. She could have returned to America, where she'd be safe, but that's never been her makeup. In school, bullies feared her. She created black eyes... body bruises... you name it. I never even *considered* talking her out of volunteering for a dangerous assignment. Being in the center of the action is where she's always strived to be. That's why she chose surgery as her nursing specialty... why she chose wartime nursing over the relative safety of a civilian hospital."

"The Eighth Army lucked out." replied 'C'.

"Teddy's a tough cookie."

* * *

May 1941

"Booty to behold," said 'C'.

The mathematicians and Alastair Denniston gazed at the paraphernalia atop the Director's desk. An open, wooden case exposed an Enigma machine, eight removable rotors, and a German code book. 'C' lifted two of the rotors out of the box, and handed them to Kenny and Alan Turing.

"This treasure trove is from a German U-boat that sank in the North Atlantic four days ago," he said. "It provides the daily rotor-setting list for an entire month or more."

"Plus insight into future lists," said Alan Turing.

"And numerous *cribs*, said Kenny.

"Fortunes of war," said Denniston.

"It came at a cost," said 'C'. "Except for the loss of life to obtain it, the Prime Minister is quite pleased about hastening America's entry into the war."

"Did they retrieve it?" asked Turing.

"A case could be made about their purposefulness," replied 'C'. "It is truly providential how God smiles down and embraces our mission? Three of our destroyers were escorting a convoy of merchant ships westbound across the Atlantic. As they neared the coast of Iceland, the U-boat fired torpedoes... and missed! Our hydrophone operators had detected its presence moments before, and the Convoy Commander issued an order for all ships to turn in tandem, forty-five degrees.

"The jig was up for the hapless boat. Our warships launched a deadly pattern of depth-charges, brought the badly-damaged U-boat to the surface to face direct fire. Point blank it was. Can you imagine? Gunnery school doesn't anticipate such simple exercises ... truly a Convoy Commander's dream. The U-boat crew abandoned ship in panic ... forgot to set the scuttling charges. Brains turned to porridge. Ha ha ha."

"How were the Americans involved?" asked Kenny.

"A small U.S. Navy vessel, a minesweeper, was clearing the port channel at Reykjavik, spotted the action on the horizon, and steamed toward it. Flag signals only ... no radio. As it got in close, one of our destroyers was picking up survivors. The U-boat was half-submerged... sinking from mortal depth-charge damage. Six crew members, wearing diving gear, from the U.S. vessel approached the distressed submarine in a rubber sea boat, and clambered aboard with hooks and netting. Without any hesitation, five Americans entered the U-boat through the open hatch... threw caution to the wind. They couldn't know what awaited them at the bottom of that ladder. Within minutes they passed these items and others topside to the sixth sailor, who'd remained there to receive them. He secured them to a line from one of our destroyers.

"Organized precision! You can't call it anything else. Without warning, the U-boat capsized... conning tower hit the water... stern raised high in the air for a brief moment... then slid downward to its watery grave. Five intrepid American sailors went down with it. The sixth man swam to the safety of his own ship. He was seen being lifted aboard."

*   *   *

"Sitting ducks in a shooting gallery," exclaimed Alastair Denniston, about the subsequent ease in decrypting German Navy intercepts.

Although the volume of intercepts increased, pressure from the Admiralty ceased. GC&CS knew what *Kriegsmarine* was planning, almost simultaneously as Nazi Navy Commanders. The mathematicians were extrapolating and estimating contents for the next *Kriegsmarine* code book from patterns, sources, and *cribs* in the documents they'd obtained from the sunken U-boat.

Roosevelt's *Lend-Lease* program was proving successful. Merchant ship convoys re-routed around discovered U-boat pack positions. Shipping losses subsided substantially.

Winston Churchill demanded copies of all decrypts—not realizing how many boxes of papers would be delivered to 10 Downing Street every single day.

'C' told top staffers that the request "will keep the Admiralty on its toes. Even if the Prime Minister doesn't read them, top brass won't know that he doesn't. If he picks and chooses, Admiralty won't know which ones. So goes away the old-school mentality that diminishes the worth of Intelligence. Bletchley Park has come into its own."

Alan Turing whispered to Kenny, "Until the *next* riddle."

*   *   *

Dear Kenny;

We have the sad news to share with you that our dear son, Darrell, drowned on May 9 in a Navy training exercise somewhere in the North Atlantic. Four others from his ship died with him. None of them have been found. Such a dangerous, yet vital, occupation is military service. Darrell truly loved it.

His mother and I are deeply appreciative of your friendship, Kenny, and the good times you and Darrell shared together at Nebraska.

Darrell was very proud to be a Navy officer and have his own ship. As are we. He loved the sea. From a very early age he surfed year-round here in Santa Barbara, and had a passion for scuba-diving up and down the California coast.

His recent bride, Lola, is pregnant. Our hearts are broken from our loss. She's inconsolable. Lola told us that if it's a boy, they had already planned to name him Albert Kenneth after his father and you—his best friend. She's been our house guest since the memorial service. God's plan is sometimes difficult to make any sense out of.

On a reminiscent note, Darrell enjoyed telling the story over and over about the Hollywood party you both attended where you multiplied two 3-digit numbers in your head before any of the film stars could do it. And they got to use pencil and paper! Most of the people he told that to didn't believe him—including his crew members. Joyce and I know it's true.

Darrell bragged to everyone that his best friend is a mathematics professor at Oxford University. That's so wonderful. We pray that you and Teddy and your faculty associates and students manage to stay as far away from the war as you can.

Please know, Kenny, that we consider you an important part of Darrell's happy and productive life. You and Teddy are always welcome as guests in our home. Thank you for being Darrell's friend and an important part of our extended family. His life was much richer for it.

Sincerely,

Albert and Joyce Cassidy
695 Cheltenham Road
Santa Barbara, California

*   *   *

Kenny could scarcely breath. He read and re-read the letter.

Nothing mattered. His best friend was dead. All of Darrell's aspirations were gone. Snuffed out—like a candle.

The letter's first sentence was a dagger.

Kenny hadn't known. Then did. Darrell's parents informed him. How difficult it must have been for them to write that sentence. He only needed to read it. Hard to do.

Kenny knew how Darrell died. And why. No one in the Cassidy family knew that. Kenny couldn't tell them. Ever.

Bletchley Park had not been privy to the names of U.S. Navy personnel drowned in the sunken U-boat off the coast of Iceland. If the United States got involved in the war, beyond *Lend-Lease*, his college pal would be recognized as one of the first casualties, but his daring feat and contribution to the war effort would remain anonymous. No medal. No citation for bravery. Acknowledging the U.S. Navy's role in the U-boat incident would belie President Roosevelt's public posture of neutrality. The ignominy of *"training accident"* would forever obscure Darrell Cassidy's biography.

What difference was there between that and the use of codes? Both served to disguise context and reality.

Kenny needed a ruse to disguise his workplace, to keep Teddy from knowing his occupation. Everyone at Bletchley Park shared that dilemma. Signing the *Official Secrets Act* mandated it.

War was indeed hell—mankind's creation that attributed no respect or meaning for human life, yet played out like a game. Politicians at military funerals claimed that it was a soldier's honor to die for his country. A more rational goal would leave the honor of dying to the enemy.

What a joke Hitler had used to rationalize his living nightmare to his countrymen. Initially, he'd claimed to covet more space for them. *Lebensraum*. That's what he called it. They believed him! By bribing his followers with that expectation, he disguised his own

purposeful zeal to rule the world. Not by mutual consent, but
by brute force. To accomplish it, he assembled a force of killers,
torturers, sadists, and millions of naïve young men, who goose-
stepped in concert to his charismatic perversion.

Darrell Cassidy had sacrificed his life to thwart them, in a single place. So had four other American sailors who followed him
down into the dark, flooding, U-boat. *Follow the leader.* That's how
they'd been trained. All had parents who loved them, brothers and
sisters, best friends, schoolmates, wives, and girlfriends who were
just as devastated about their loss as Kenny and Darrell's parents.
Memorial services in four cities, besides Santa Barbara, were filled
with grief-stricken, shocked mourners. Darrell Cassidy's death left
an emptiness in their lives. None were told about the five sailors'
brave action—only that they'd served their country honorably.

* * *

Loneliness followed Kenny around. His house in Teddington
was empty every night, upon his arrival from Bletchley Park—and
during his infrequent days off. Breakfast and dinner chatter with
Teddy about hospital happenings were no more. He learned to
cook what he liked, and ate alone. Whenever he motorcycled past
the hospital, he imagined her toiling in the operating room, or
peeking through a window at him. Nurses walking alongside the
road recognized him and waved. None were ever Teddy.

He had no inkling about when he'd see her again. Long ab-
sences had been emphasized by the recruiters when she was mull-
ing over military nursing. Local billeting had not been promised—
instead, a strong likelihood for the contrary. They'd showcased
Army nurses serving during the Great War. No one predicted a
short assignment.

Loneliness was not the same as having regrets. He had none. At least he'd been successful convincing himself to believe that. Being left behind during wartime was no different for him than it would have been for her being the one left behind. Hundreds of thousands of families throughout Great Britain were facing similar separations. He'd been restrained by the *Official Secrets Act* about confiding to Teddy that he was already serving.

Alan Turing pointed out the irony. "You're both fighting the Nazis *and* being left behind," he said.

Letters from Teddy usually arrived in rubber-banded bundles of six to ten at a time. All were postmarked with an Eighth Army imprint, but their circuitous route from somewhere in Egypt to England always took a week or two for delivery to Teddington. Kenny had asked her to write candidly—and she did.

*

My Dearest Kenny,

I will not ever be able to tell you where I am, but I feel safe and in good hands. I love you very much. I take great comfort every day knowing that you are not assigned to a tank crew here in the African desert.

My field hospital is set up inside the rear lines, but within thirty minutes of the front lines, by ambulance.

To an outsider it resembles bedlam, but we are amazingly organized. Triage works well, thank heavens. Army medics are well-trained. My team consists of the most amazing and talented surgeons! No procedure is beyond their skill. Following major surgeries, patients are flown out, when flights are available. Others go to one of our 25-bed wards, each in one of twenty-four separate tents. Pretty huge, huh? We have more capacity than London General. Our two operating room theater tents are linked with a square tent in the middle for sterilizing. We receive several truckloads of medical supplies every week.

We have already relocated once since I arrived. We just pick up and go—"patients, kit, and kaboodle!" (one colonel's favorite expression) With only thirty minutes advance notice. It's organized chaos. Just like a traveling circus. Can you imagine? And it takes so little time. General Montgomery knows what he's doing. I got to meet him. He thanked me for volunteering. Everyone refers to him as Monty.

It's always dusty here in the desert from constant wind and vehicle movement. It gets into everything. The terrain is very flat and hot. We keep the sand and huge mosquitoes away the best we can with netting, and operate with portable lights most of the time. Sometimes with hurricane lamps during a blackout. I've attended surgeons removing shrapnel, with only a flashlight.

We work 2/12's. That's twelve hours on duty, twelve hours off, though we work lots of our off-hours. We share sleeping quarters. Two nurses per belle tent. My current tent-mate snores just like you. I know—I know! You don't snore! Ha!

Your photograph sits atop my military-issue valise beside my cot. It's just big enough to pack a blanket, pillow, wooden tripod, camp bed, and canvas wash basin into. We practiced that at Orientation. All the comforts of home, huh?

Pray for the defeat of German Field Marshal Rommel. That's who the Eighth Army is after. I see his picture taped to dart boards. Hitler, too. We won't have to work so hard when it happens.

I hope you are getting lots of sleep and eating well. When you make your pancakes, don't forget to add a teaspoon of baking powder to the batter. Don't worry about me, my dearest Kenny. The food is quite good here. Your beautiful, adoring wife never lost a fight. General Montgomery knows what he's doing.

Love and kisses,

Teddy

Chapter Twenty-one

It was ironic that the German encryption system utilized in Italy, Africa, and the Mediterranean had been invented by British Intelligence during the Great War. *Enigma— it* was not. Something entirely different.

Conceivably, the Nazis believed it had been long forgotten, but, more likely, Hitler's arrogance about German superiority in all things human induced him to risk devising confounding improvements and complications, and defeat the English with England's own, long-dormant creation. Another possibility was that Benito Mussolini, Italy's dictator and one of Hitler's strongest European allies, preferred its basic simplicity and ease of mastering for usage on the battlefield.

Playfair was its name.

'C' indicated that he wasn't sure which motive was relevant, if any, but he'd become aware of its use in the Mediterranean several months before the autumn of 1941, and ordered a Special Section to be set up in one of several newly-constructed Huts outside the Bletchley Park mansion to give it undivided attention. Kenny got transferred to the *Playfair* Hut from the Cottage. For the first time since his arrival at Bletchley Park, he was not partnered with Alan Turing.

* * *

"We still need a minimum of eighty intercepts each day for odds improvement," said Kenny, "plus the help of the *Bombe* machines, to unravel myriad variables. Then, this riddle begins.

"He stood in front of an assemblage of thirty Enigma-experienced individuals he'd selected from other Bletchley Park Huts for his new assignment. It was their first day. They filled every job description required for the *Playfair* challenge.

'C' had given him the authority to cherry-pick whomever he wanted from the various Huts, provided he took no more than four (including clerks) from any of them. Naturally, there was resistance by the leaders of those Huts. His top choices included a recently-recruited mathematics professor from Oxford University, Dr. John Thornton, as his Chief Assistant; Royal Navy captain, Sean Devereux, as Watch Commander; and Royal Army lieutenant colonel, Patrick O'Doherty, as Assistant Watch Commander.

On the blackboard, Kenny printed a 5 x 5 *grid* of letters. "Welcome to *Playfair* 101," he said. "Think of today as a super-condensed university course for the basic understanding of *Playfair*. Tell me what you see... anyone?"

K R O N E
L D T A B
C F G H I
M P Q S U
V W X Y Z

"Five code-groups, stacked vertically," said one.

"To an outsider, it's an eye chart," said another.

Everyone laughed.

"It spells out your last name, Professor," said a Navy Wren, "followed by the remaining alphabet… in order… without duplicating any letter in your name. A letter is missing. It's J."

"Absolutely correct," replied Kenny. "*KRONELDT* is spelled out on the first two lines of the *grid*. That represents the keyword. Question. Suppose we do not know what the keyword is?"

"That will be our job, won't it?" asked another. "To determine what it is?"

Kenny smiled. "You are making me a happy man. Question. What if the remaining letters following the keyword are not in alphabetical order?"

"Can we presume the Italians and Germans have added that difficulty to Playfair?" asked a uniformed Naval officer.

"I am feeling even better," replied Kenny. "Think of yourselves as a code encrypter at an Italian military command in Sicily, and you are sending this message." He printed it on the blackboard. Laughing occurred.

HITLER WILL LOSE

"Looking at the message in *bigrams*, it becomes…" He printed it directly underneath.

HI TL ER WI LL LO SE.

"Each pair of letters is substituted by another pair. Here's how. If letters in a pair are on the same row, move each letter to the right. H and I are in the third row, so H becomes I, and I becomes

C, because a letter at the end of a row jumps to the front of that same row. Thus, IC becomes the substitution for HI."

```
K R O N E
L D T A B
C F G HI
M P Q S U
V W X Y Z
```

"If both letters are in the same vertical column, and one of them is at the bottom, it jumps up to the top.

"TL is the next *bigram*. Both letters are on the same row in the *grid*, so the T becomes A, and L becomes D. Thus, AD is substituted for TL."

```
K R O N E
L D T A B
C F G H I
M P Q S U
V W X Y Z
```

"Same with the third *bigram*, ER. E becomes K, because… being at the end of the row, it moves to the front of the row. R becomes O… it moves to the right. Thus, ER becomes KO.

"WI is different, because those two letters are on different rows and columns in the *grid*. Look at them as corners of a rectangle that are diagonal from each other. The opposite corners of that rectangle are F and Z. So, W becomes F, and I becomes Z. Thus, WI becomes FZ."

K R O N E
L D T A B
C F G H **I**
M P Q S U
V **W** X Y Z

"LL becomes DD. Remember… move one space to the right. LO is another rectangle. Look at the opposite corners. L becomes K, and O becomes T. Thus, LO becomes KT."

K R **O** N E
L D T A B
C F G H I
M P Q S U
V W X Y Z

"SE is also a rectangle. Opposite corners are N and U, so SE becomes NU."

K R O N **E**
L D T A B
C F G H I
M P Q **S** U
V W X Y Z

Kenny printed the substitution *bigrams* under the originals as he spoke.

HI TL ER WI LL LO SE.
IC AD KO FZ DD KT NU

"The *Playfair* message is sent by radio in the same format as what you've been used to, with Enigma intercepts... five-letter code-groups... like this."

ICADK OFZDD KTNU(**Q**)

"A randomly-selected letter, in this example... a Q, is added for filler at the end to form a five-letter code-group, if necessary."

Kenny nodded at Captain Devereux to speak. Without hesitation, the Navy officer strode up to the front of the room.

"Professor Kroneldt has just given you the elementary lowdown," he said, "but recent alterations by the enemy have made it more testing. Not only do they *randomly* distribute the alphabet in their *grids*, but they're currently utilizing *two grids* for each message. Each requires a separate keyword. They change them every day. Does Professor Kroneldt look concerned about that? Noooo! Not on your life. That's why 'C' selected him to head up this Hut... and why the Professor selected each of you. Professor Kroneldt hand-picked each and every one of us for this important task. If Rommel only knew what's in store for him.

"The *Playfair* code is laborious and mistake-prone at both ends... encryptions and decryptions. When the enemy makes a mistake, he will need to re-send it. Corrupted messages are worthless to them. Based on our experience with Enigma intercepts, that will occur frequently... and greatly assist us in our endeavor. From our end, we cannot afford to make mistakes. *Playfair* Hut will be crackerjack."

* * *

December 7, 1941

Jane was awakened by her telephone. It was Sunday. She hoped it would stop ringing, but it didn't. She finally picked up the receiver.

"Have you heard the news?" asked a keyed-up, female voice. It was Gladys Rogel. "Jane... have you heard the news? The Japanese just bombed Pearl Harbor! It was announced on the radio!"

"The Japanese just bombed what?" She rubbed her eyes.

"Pearl Harbor! It's a huge Navy Base in Hawaii. The Japanese bombed it today... this morning! Many ships were sunk... surprise attack... hundreds of servicemen are dead... they don't know how many... it may still be going on. Jack Wagner just spoke to Clive on the phone... he shut down production for next week. Governor Olson declared a blackout starting tonight in all cities and towns along the coast. Los Angeles Mayor Bowron asked that people avoid driving at night, if at all possible... no one knows what's happening... why don't you come and stay with us for a few days?"

"You and Clive can stay with me," replied Jane.

"Jack wants to talk to you and a few others... he says the subject is urgent and can't wait... he and Clive are calling people right now... the meeting is at our home here in Studio City at two o'clock... it's hush-hush... that's why it's here... Jack needs you to come, Jane, please tell me you can."

* * *

"Our boys will now be in this war... tens of thousands of them," said Jack Wagner, "and during their rests between battles, we need to be there with them."

A group of stage, screen, and radio headliners showed up to join him and Jane in the spacious patio of the Rogel home. Included were Mickey Rooney, Bing Crosby, Bob Hope, Chico Marx, Judy Garland, Spike Jones, Nelson Eddy, Tommy Dorsey, Glenn Miller, Kay Kyser, Stan Laurel, Oliver Hardy, Errol Flynn, Edgar Bergen, Ann Sheridan, Martha Raye, Ray Bolger, John Garfield, Xavier Cugat, Benny Goodman, and Marlene Dietrich.

"The President will speak to Congress tomorrow," said Errol Flynn, "to announce a conscription plan, undoubtedly?"

"Of course," replied Marlene Dietrich. "But, thousands will volunteer, and not wait to be drafted."

"Young and old alike," said Judy Garland.

"We realized months ago that war with Germany was inevitable." said Wagner. "Pretending otherwise wouldn't change anything. Japan was a surprise. We need to expedite."

"Tell us why you called us here," said Mickey Rooney.

"Camp Shows, Incorporated..." replied Jack Wagner, "that's our official name ... under the broad umbrella of *United Service Organizations*. We've already got the green light from the White House. Harry Hopkins, one of President Roosevelt's advisors, suggested *USO* for our acronym... easy to say, remember, and publicize. I've been an active member of the *Citizens Committee For the Army and Navy*. We've been organizing, behind the scenes, since late last year."

"Who's we?" asked Glenn Miller.

"Producers, agents, studio executives, Broadway angels... here and New York. I'm involved in the *Hollywood Committee* branch.

"Pretty good at keeping secrets," said John Garfield.

"President Roosevelt needed to appear neutral to assure his re-election," replied Wagner. "Today's attack on Pearl Harbor changes all that. We are now at war and can go public with our plans, following his speech to Congress tomorrow."

"What's our role?" asked Spike Jones.

"Commit to small-ensemble variety shows... complete with live music ... everywhere our Army and Navy goes, including boot camps, military bases, Navy ships, airfields, battle areas, you name it. We plan to open *Stage Door Canteens* in New York City and Hollywood right away. We'll open *Canteens* in other military towns as fast as we can get them ready. Soldiers, sailors, airmen, and marines can dance, relax, be treated like the important individuals that they are... where they'll get to meet a show business luminary or two."

"This can't diminish our popularity," said Stan Laurel, "while enhancing our military warriors' stature."

"You sure said a mouthful," replied Oliver Hardy. He rolled up his sleeves and flexed his muscles.

Laurel stared at him with wide eyes, then at everyone.

"What about our film commitments?" asked Ann Sheridan. "Some of us are contract players."

"I'll see that there's time for both," replied Wagner. "Motion pictures will have a different emphasis. Features and documentaries will support the war effort... stories of heroism, sacrifice, honor, patriotism, duty. I've been compiling a selection of scripts."

Chapter Twenty-two

JUNE 1942

How could one individual mount such worldwide devastation and peril, Kenny wondered? Right under everybody's noses.

Was it obvious to some at the present time, only because it was actually happening, or was Hitler's menace foreseen years earlier? It was so blatantly obvious to Kenny's University of Nebraska professor colleagues in 1933. They'd railed against Hitler's book-burnings, banning of Jews and journalists, Gestapo, concentration camps, brownshirts, and execution of University of Munich students, who'd opposed Nazism.

When Winston Churchill—as a House of Lords member—had spoken out against Neville Chamberlain's appeasement-at-all-costs activities, he was shouted down in Parliament, then ridiculed in the press as "*anti-peace* and a War-Lord."

Kenny believed that President Roosevelt feigned *neutrality,* to win votes from the peace advocates during his 1940 re-election campaign against Wendell Wilkie.

Was it a higher priority to win an election than to defeat Hitler? Did the cause for *any* delay in a U.S. military alliance with Britain matter? Only Roosevelt and God knew the answers, but the questions haunted Kenny, nevertheless. He'd been teased about it from time to time by his Bletchley Park associates—including Alastair Denniston and 'C'.

Britain had carried on the fight against the Nazis alone. Fortunately, *Lend-Lease* came along, but it might have come months earlier, along with overt military involvement and a switchover to a wartime manufacturing economy in the United States, without Roosevelt's ambivalent motive.

Kenny didn't pretend to know how national leaders made decisions, or how they weighed the pros and cons of their diverse constituencies, but he recognized the irony that America had finally jumped into the cesspool of war, as a direct result of Japan's attack on Pearl Harbor—not by anything Hitler was doing. Kenny had several years advantage of deciphering diplomatic and military intercepts, from both sides, to form his judgment.

Perhaps, politicians' reluctance to confront such apparent evil was due to their incredulity that God could have allowed a monster like Adolf Hitler to be born. Were the aberrations of human procreation such that, once every billion births or so, the mix of genes and chromosomes in one unfortunate fetus could be so horribly malformed as to create such a creature—who'd motivate a legion of acquiescent, unquestioning followers that willingly carried out his broad menu of criminalities with such cold brutality and single-mindedness?

Germans elected Hitler president in 1933. While promising voters he'd overcome the Depression, stimulate the economy back into full production and employment, deal with the labor unions, and expand living space for Germanic citizens, he persuaded surrounding European nations that his goal was mutual peace and prosperity.

He lied.

His land grab—under the perverted umbrella of *Leben-sraum*—beginning with Austria, was followed by Sudetenland, Czechoslovakia, Poland, Holland, Belgium, Norway, and France. Next, the planet?

Hitler wasn't playing solitary. Already he'd recruited Benito Mussolini of Italy and Tojo—Japan's Prime Minister—to be his warring partners for world domination. Kenny couldn't help wondering whether the three even trusted each other, and what their own secret motives were for participating in the trio. Wouldn't it be fitting if each of them planned to dispose of the other two when the time was right? Surely, the Italian and Japanese leaders couldn't believe that Hitler would share equal power with them in victory.

Potential opponents such as Russia's Josef Stalin and England's Neville Chamberlain were temporarily neutralized by him before the war's onset with separate peace pacts. But, following the Pearl Harbor attack, Winston Churchill was angling to persuade the skeptical Stalin that Russia would soon follow, although intercepts at Bletchley Park revealed that the Communist leader was waiting to see "where the wind was blowing." 'C' referred to him as a "political opportunist and fair weather friend."

* * *

The doorbell rang. Kenny strode from his breakfast table and opened the door. 'C' stood alone on the porch, holding his ever-present cigar.

"I realize today is one of your rare days off," he said, "but I need to have a word with you in private."

"Let's talk over fresh coffee in the kitchen," replied Kenny, as he led the way and seated his guest at the table.

"You and your Americans." 'C' laughed.

"Morning, noon, and night," replied Kenny. "Alan Turing and I always had a pot brewing in the cottage. He acquired his addiction at Princeton. Now, the crew in Playfair Hut is acquiring a taste for it. Tea consumption is down." He poured two fresh cups and sat down.

"Since yesterday morning," said 'C', "the U.S. Navy scored a huge victory by sinking four Japanese carriers at Midway Island in the Pacific. Signals Intelligence played a huge role informing the American Admirals, Nimitz and Spruance, where major elements of Yamamoto's fleet lurked."

"What part of the world isn't being drawn into war?"

"Winston Churchill has been pressuring me to share our Intelligence methods with the Americans."

"We invent ruses to disguise how we obtain information.

Wouldn't spreading it over a broader base risk compromising our operation?"

"Hitler and his cronies don't know the existence of Bletchley Park, or that we are even aware of their Enigma machines. They'd be shocked out of their woolies if they discovered how we know what they're up to?"

"How good *is* American Intelligence?"

"Turf battles. OP-20-G at Arlington Hall in Washington interpreted recent Japanese intercepts as a second attack on Hawaii... or the Johnston Islands, seven hundred-fifty miles distant. Their radio Intelligence Station Hypo in Honolulu had deduced from the same intercepts that the target would be Midway. OP-20--G is already taking credit for it, and undermining the real codebreakers. If Nimitz and Spruance had sprung for Arlington Hall's interpretation, Midway Island would be occupied by the Japanese right now."

"Have you made a decision about the Prime Minister's request?"

"The Americans are sending over a contingent of their Military Intelligence experts to discuss the matter. That's one reason I came here today. You're my solo American scientist at Bletchley Park. Thank God you're here. To be candid, I've been equivocating between hiding you or putting you on display. It's your choice, Professor. You have the option of being involved in the meetings... or not."

"Can we trust their discretion?"

"I'll let you know when they arrive."

*   *   *

Kenny understood the philosophical and practical conflicts about sharing Intelligence secrets and sources with allies—from both the British and American points of view. There was general paranoia on both sides.

He realized if he'd never left Nebraska, and only heard simplistic arguments by U.S. political and military leaders—along with news reports—he'd agree, enthusiastically, that sources should be shared. Britain had been fighting the Nazis since 1939, and had a track record of Intelligence breakthroughs and *same-day* decryptions. America wanted to catch up. *Sharing* would accomplish that for them.

However, he *did* leave Nebraska, and was deeply immersed in Britain's Intelligence programs, not only as a participant, but as one of the principal problem-solvers, and he knew only too well how easily all the good work of Bletchley Park would be invalidated, and caused to become ineffective, if leaks, indiscretions, breaks in security, counterintelligence agents, moles, gossip, bad luck, laziness, or simple carelessness intervened. Britain displayed the good sense and foresight to require every staffer—regardless of civilian or military rank—to sign the *Official Secrets Act*. No one could even disclose his job to a family member! People had a natural and favorable bias toward the side on which they knew the players and systems—but skepticism toward the other, on which they did not.

* * *

Kenny could see that 'C' was walking a tightrope between telling the contingent of U.S. Intelligence experts everything, without *telling them everything*. The venue was Whitehall, not Bletchley Park, for the two-day event.

A fortnight had elapsed since the Prime Minister's initial *sharing* request. The American group, consisting of a 2-star general, vice-admiral, Navy captain, Army colonel, and four aides, had flown to London, protected by fighter plane escorts from aircraft carriers along the way. The show of top brass indicated high priority.

It became obvious during each American participant's opening remarks that they wanted to centralize—thus control—signals Intelligence at Arlington Hall in Washington, D.C. Perhaps, asking for too much was their ploy to get other important concessions. But 'C', who hosted the event, had his own major concerns—*security and secrecy*—and he made them the first topics on the agenda.

"The more widespread the existence of our systems becomes known, the more likelihood of discovery by our common enemy," he told them.

The British group included Denniston and Turing.

"Rest assured," replied the General. "We have put together the best security measures in the world to guarantee that our dealings together will be top secret. You'll be convinced of that by the time we leave tomorrow."

"Speaking for the U.S. Navy, I ditto that," said the Vice-Admiral. "Moreover, just in the past two weeks…"

"Excuse me, Admiral," said 'C'. He waved a decrypt over his head. "This arrived early this morning. It contains the transcript of a newspaper article from yesterday's *New York Times*. Let me read an excerpt.

> *"Colonel William "Wild Bill" Donovan has a new hush-hush mission—to supervise the United States Secret Service and ally it with the British Secret Service… The American 'Mr. X', as he is know privately, will report directly to the President."'*

Stony silence followed.

"It wasn't exactly *hush-hush* by the time the reporter got through with it, now was it, Colonel Donovan?" he asked. "Do you suppose the reporter made this all up by himself, and now, here you are?"

'C' peered into his briefcase and pulled out an issue of the *Chicago Tribune*. "Here's another… about Midway… Navy this time. The headline reads, 'NAVY HAD WORD OF JAP PLAN TO STRIKE AT SEA.' Can you imagine what I would do to the person who leaked a story like this here in England? How does it help our war effort? Perhaps the thinking was that Japs don't read the *Chicago Tribune*. Or more naive, they have no agents in Illinois. Or possibly, spies don't have access to that publication. The story was picked up by newspapers in Washington and New York and God knows how many other cities and towns! I'll read part of it to you.

> *"The strength of the Japanese forces, with which the American Navy is battling somewhere West of Midway Island in what is believed to be the greatest Naval battle of the war, was well known in American Naval circles, several days before the battle began, reliable sources in Naval Intelligence disclosed here tonight.'*

"Reliable? To whom? The newspaper reporter? The Navy? The war effort? Americans? Brits? I defy anyone to find any stories like this in any British newspaper. Discretion is more than rhetoric. *Secrecy* deserves a better definition than simply being a 7-letter or 3-syllable word.

"Our conference over the next two days will bear fruit and a meaningful outcome, gentlemen. Your journey here will not be for naught, but we must avoid discovery and self-deception at all costs."

*   *   *

Kenny knew 'C's argument would prevail. After all, Britain had the proven methodologies, Enigma replicas, Bombes, experience in their use, *cribs* library, established location, trained staff, and well-honed operation. Why build another mousetrap, when the best mousetrap already existed?

Moreover, the U.S. contingent could not point out any British security breaches—and it was difficult for them to disagree that secrecy was the top priority. If anything, the humbled Americans were glaring at each other for "loose lips"—as 'C' had characterized the principal reason for same.

The event was expanded to five days, after *rules* were crafted and agreed upon for handling the newly-named, *Special Intelligence*—also referred to as *high-grade intercepts* and *machine ciphers*. Bletchley Park Intelligence was designated *Ultra*; Arlington Hall's and outlet stations—*Zymotic*.

RULES FOR HANDLING ULTRA

1. Utmost secrecy must always be used in dealing with Special Intelligence. If from any captured document, intercepted message, prisoner of war examination, or ill-considered action based on Special Intelligence, enemy suspect, source would instantaneously cease probably forever.

2. Any breach would vitally affect operations on all fronts, not only that on which you command.

3. Avoid giving information as Intelligence to lower commands, use only for passing operational order to lower commands. If

*passing Intelligence is unavoidable, make
no reference to secret source. Use only prefix
ULTRA. Such messages only to be handed to
and deciphered by designated officer, using
only highest grade cipher; no record of messages is to be kept at Forward Commands.
Messages to be destroyed by fire when read;
same for ships at sea.*

*4. In briefing pilots, only use Intelligence
essential to success of operation. Strive to
use information from other sources whenever possible.*

*5. If any action is based on source, lo-
cal Commander must ensure action can-
not be traced to source alone. MOMEN-
TARY TACTICAL ADVANTAGE NOT
WORTH RISK OF COMPROMISING
SOURCE.*

*6. No reference to this information is to be
made in summaries, however limited the
circulation. No discussion of it.*

Alastair Denniston, Alan Turing, and Kenny led the visitors
on a selective and tightly-controlled tour of Bletchley Park, which
had grown to more than a thousand staffers in eight separate Huts,
mansion, and numerous outlying buildings in recent months.

In the Bombe Hut, Alan Turing and Kenny took turns explaining the
intricacies of the machines, and Bletchley Park's need for thirty more.

"The daily volume of intercepts has become horrendous," said Turing, "as you could see in the various Huts."

"Full-tilt, twenty-four hours a day," said Denniston.

"Bombe machine production might be an area for American assistance," said Turing. "We have the blueprints, your technical machine manufacturers have the production capabilities."

"IBM or National Cash Register would be good vendors," replied Colonel Donovan. "They can produce Arlington Hall's requirements at the same time."

"I believe we can get that handled under provisions of Lend-Lease," said the 2-Star General.

"No question about it," replied Colonel Donovan.

"We'll provide technical assistance," said Denniston.

"How long have you been involved, Dr. Kroneldt?" asked the Vice-Admiral.

"I was recruited here from Nebraska in 1937."

"How did they find out about you?"

"Good grades in college… mathematics and physics."

"Are you married?"

"To my childhood sweetheart."

"An English girl?"

"American… my wife is from Chicago."

"Did she return there after the outbreak?"

"She's a Royal Army nurse in Egypt."

"I see."

Chapter Twenty-three

Regardless of how much talent German Field Marshal Erwin Rommel had as a tactician and military leader, without gasoline for his tanks, he was dead in his tracks.

Breakthroughs in signals intelligence, transmitted from Italy, Egypt, Libya, and the Mediterranean, provided Kenny's Playfair Hut consistent insights and precise data about German cargo ship movements and Rommel's order of battle. Royal Air Force torpedo-bombers and British submarines awaited at anticipated locations for the doomed vessels, then pounced with pinpoint precision, while Rommel and his frustrated commanders suffered diminishing gas supplies and empty docks at African port cities.

Kenny had fun inventing ruses. They included nonexistent British Armies. At a staff meeting with 'C', he proposed a fictitious Zee Force. Military commanders opted to compose it with two, non-existent, armored divisions, five infantry divisions, and a Corps Headquarters—somewhere in the Sahara Desert. Tents and tanks were represented by cardboard cutouts, to deceive high-altitude, reconnaissance aircraft.

"The Germans developed Enigma," he proclaimed, "so they're smart enough to break the Zee Force code. Hitler and his intelligence people surely wonder how we know so much about their ships in the Mediterranean. Why not divert their attention to the equally important subject of Rommel's imminent peril? Evading the decoy army will require Hitler's favorite Field Marshal to use up his remaining fuel."

"Ha ha ha. Your thinking is both strategic and tactical," replied C'. "It's a wonder you became an academic... and not a military man."

"Rommel surely knows the history of Lawrence of Arabia," said Denniston, "the role-model for Kroneldt's creation."

"General Montgomery plays that part well," replied a Royal Army colonel.

"On a broader scale," said Denniston, "the Royal Navy is feinting an operation in the Baltic to divert the *Luftwaffe* and *Kreigsmarine* away from the Africa campaign."

"It's all working," said 'C'. "Montgomery brought Rommel to a complete stop at Alam el Halfa. El Alamein is crucial to victory in Africa."

* * *

Kenny never mentioned Teddy at any Intelligence meetings, but he suspected all attendees knew she stood in harm's way. Of course, all of them did, too. The Germans could bomb Bletchley Park out of existence, if they knew about it. Spies were suspected to be everywhere. Paranoia reigned.

V-2 rockets terrorized Londoners most nights. Everyone had a gas mask—babies included. Citizens knew where the bomb shelters were. Many felt responsible for the safety of a neighborhood family, co-worker, or friend. Air raid sirens were scary. Bomb shelters filled quickly. People made room. They whispered, and babies cried.

V-2 rockets made a receding, whistling sound, as they passed by overhead or dropped from the sky, close by—followed by a second or two of silence—then a deafening roar, causing violent vibrations that shook loose paint chips, litter, and dust from the shelter ceiling and walls, and moved the occupied benches a few centimeters. Strangers gripped onto each other.

Distant bombs hit the ground with resounding thuds, emulating elephants fainting on the back porch. Views of the horizon provided pulsating flashes, klieg lights searching the night sky for aircraft, raging fires, smoke, and destruction.

*   *   *

Kenny could only imagine Teddy gazing outward from her hospital tent at Rommel's Panzer tanks on a faraway sandy bluff, overlooking her position.

"They've stopped!" shouted an unfamiliar voice from beside her. "They've all stopped! Monty told us they'd run out of gas, and they did!"

*   *   *

USO duty was exhilarating for Jane, but full of stress.

At the outset, she'd been given her choice of European or Pacific venues, and she'd chosen the former, in accompaniment with bandleader, Nelson Eddy, Chico Marx, Edgar Bergen, and Marlene Dietrich. The troupe included band members, two writers, and several equipment handlers.

After performing for packed audiences at three Army forts, a Marine training base, and two Naval Stations between Florida and Maine—constantly updating their repertoires, musical selections, and staging—they traveled together to undisclosed European destinations to entertain American, British, and Allied troops. They didn't know where they were most of the time, nor did they ask, remaining just long enough at each location to do a show. The entertainers were constantly on the move, fully aware of the dangers. Sounds of battle emanated from nearby hills, so close were they to the front lines.

Edgar Bergen created a Hitler puppet that always got outsmarted by counter-intelligence agent, *Charlie McCarthy*, then ridiculed by "German Colonel", *Mortimer Snerd*, whose lack of common sense was exceeded only by Hitler's. Chico Marx portrayed a lascivious, lusting, Nazi, Romeo-in-waiting to Marlene Dietrich's and Jane's femmes fatale, whose double entendre song lyrics brought wildly-cheering audiences to their feet.

Accommodations were Spartan: lavatories… portable; dressing rooms… canvas walls; costumes… military garb. No one desired to return home early. All voted to extend the tour. Dozens of other USO troupes did the same.

*   *   *

When Marlene Dietrich and Jane had been exclusively invited together into the Command Tent, following one of the mid-tour USO performances, they knew it wasn't for an obligatory "meet everybody in charge" social hour—along with a positive recap of the war. Those always included every troupe member.

Canvas chairs faced a makeshift movie screen pinned to the canvas wall. A film projector was already threaded—ready to show. Several Army officers stood to greet them and exchange pleasantries.

"We found this recently-produced propaganda film in the knapsack of a captured, Nazi SS officer," said the Colonel-in-Charge, after all were seated. The performers sat in front. "The setting is claimed to be a Jewish settlement in Theresienstadt, a small town in German-occupied Czechoslovakia. If you feel comfortable translating, Miss Dietrich, I invite you to do so. Be prepared for a shock."

The show's title flashed onto the screen.

Theresienstadt Sonderbehandlung:

Ein Dokumentarfilm aus dem Judischen Siedlungsgebiet 1936-1944.

"Theresienstadt Special Treatment: A Documentary Film of the Jewish Resettlement 1936-1944," recited Marlene Dietrich.

A montage of resident activities included: tea-time in the courtyard at sun-shaded tables; families enjoying ping pong, billiards, horseshoes, card games, shuffleboard, and splashing in the pool; dining together beside a well-stocked smorgasbord; unpacking clothes in spacious closets; a children's choir performing with an orchestra in a packed theater; et al. A soft-speaking male narrated, voice-over, as Marlene Dietrich interpreted aloud.

"This is Theresienstadt... a peaceful, comfortable retreat for Jewish families to live free from the war in safety and harmony."

Jane stood up and screamed. "That voice... it's Klaus's voice... that's Klaus Leonhardt... that's his voice... I'd know it anywhere... he's alive... Klaus is alive." She couldn't take her eyes off the screen.

At that moment, her frail-looking, but smiling, fiancé looked up from the billiards table in the film. His casual clothing was apropos for yachting or tennis.

"Look! It's him… it's Klaus," she said. "He's so thin… but he's my Klaus!"

"Greetings, my Jewish friends," intoned Marlene Dietrich, still interpreting the dialogue. "I am Klaus Leonhardt. You know me from my film roles. I am anxious to know you…"

Jane fainted.

* * *

She awakened on a cot. Someone had placed a folded-up blanket under her head and a wet towel on her forehead. She heard voices, but didn't open her eyes.

"How many of these *Jewish settlements* are there?" asked Marlene Dietrich.

"We're aware of prison-of-war camps, called *stalags* or concentration camps, Miss Dietrich," replied the Colonel, "but no *Jewish settlements*, as such, other than *Theresientadt*."

"The film was staged," said Dietrich. "My friend, Kurt Gerron, was credited as the Director. I've known him since he began his career as a gifted performer. It looks like his work. They've got him, too. Kurt Gerron could have come to America with *me*. Everyone in this fraudulent production was posed for dramatic camera shots… the lighting, theatrical… yet, no one was wearing jewelry, not even a timepiece… restraint impeded their movement… their comments, stilted… fear glowered through the smiles on their faces, particularly the children's."

"The SS officer professed to know nothing about it."

"Wouldn't you say nothing, too?"

"The film shows Klaus Leonhardt is alive. We wanted Miss Palmer to see it."

"Can you estimate, from the various buildings in the film, how many Jews are in there?"

"Three thousand… four thousand, just a guess."

"What about the others?"

"What others?"

"The five to six million missing Jews, Colonel. They haven't turned up anywhere. Did they go poof? Gone! Poof! Like puffs of smoke. Poof!

"I wish we knew."

"The Nazis have murdered the Jews, Colonel. Every one that they rounded up. They've been murdering Jews since Hitler took over… thousands at a time. Haven't you heard Hitler's proclamations about his *master race?*"

"How could they hide so many?"

"In mass graves, of course."

"That would be unprecedented evil," replied the Colonel. "Surely, you exaggerate. Those that haven't already fled Europe could be in other *Jewish settlements.*"

"How many so-called *Jewish settlements,* with an estimated capacity of three or four thousand, would it take to hide five or six million missing Jews? Is everyone blind to what has been going on? Tell me, Colonel. Are you?"

"*Theresienstadt* is the only *Jewish settlement* we are aware of, Miss Dietrich."

"Isn't it apparent that Hitler and his chief propagandist, Goering, have kept Klaus Leonhardt alive only to make propaganda films?"

*   *   *

When Jane awakened in the morning it was raining. She couldn't distinguish between her dread of consciousness and nightmares. The warm glow of confirmation that her fiancé had survived alternated with the fearsome thought that he might soon be dead—if not already. Military commanders had repeatedly warned that targeting prisoner-of-war camps could jeopardize all the inmates, just as an assault on *Theresienstadt* would do the same. Doing nothing maintained the status quo. Choosing the latter was deemed wiser than risking sure death for captives in the crossfire. Repatriation could occur at war's end.

During a pre-dawn breakfast she didn't let on that she'd overheard the conversation between Marlene Dietrich and the Colonel. Nor did she even mention Klaus Leonhardt's name. She surmised from their silence that others who'd attended the previous night's meeting had been sworn to secrecy. When she'd emerged earlier from her tent, the Colonel informed her confidentially that the captured film would not be disseminated, nor would he alert the press about Klaus Leonhardt being alive.

"That could endanger him more," he said.

Jane's conundrum: if she went public with the news, the Nazis would kill him immediately, to avoid admitting that he was their prisoner—*and* to keep him from talking about the true horrors at the *settlement*; if she didn't, they would kill him, anyway, before the war ended—for the same reasons. The film was done. What else did they need him for? She believed Marlene Dietrich's assertion that the Nazis had already murdered millions of Jews. How else could their absence be explained?

Chapter Twenty-four

The Bletchley Park bulletin board was getting crowded with codebreaking-initiated victories against the Nazis in recent months. Kenny and other staffers crowded around it every day for a look-see. Most were banner-headlined stories from British newspapers, and transcripts of radio broadcasts.

ROMMEL ROUTED IN TUNISIA

ALLIES LAND IN NORTH AFRICA

GERMANS CAPITULATE AT STALINGRAD

U-BOATS EXIT NORTH ATLANTIC

MONTGOMERY & PATTON LIBERATE SICILY

HITLER ASSASSINATION ATTEMPT FAILS

D-DAY AT NORMANDY - EISENHOWER PRAISED

PARIS LIBERATED - DEGAULLE RETURNS

GERMANY CAUGHT IN ALLIED'S PINCER

For only the second time since the war began, 'C' posted a declassified secret document—along with a list of Nazi concentration camps—on the Bletchley Park bulletin board, and required all 2000+ staffers to attend a reading of them on the mansion lawn, before or after their shifts. He repeated his presentation morning and afternoon. Kenny attended the first one. Following each, 'C' simply drove away in his Lancia convertible.

"No one knows better than you the horrors of this war and the vicious tactics of the Nazis," proclaimed 'C' from an elevated platform. "Many of you have lost a brother, sister, nephew, niece, uncle, father, son, daughter, friend, neighbor, classmate, former colleague. Some, more than one.

"Even now, with the Nazis on the run, V-2 rockets are raining down each night upon innocent civilians in London and environs. What I am about to read to you is the horror story of all horror stories. The Nazis have been committing unspeakable acts against humankind... against an entire race of people, the Jews! We obtained this letter, written in 1942, from a captured enemy agent, along with this recently-obtained list of Nazi concentration camps. Why the good Lord didn't put this information into our hands sooner, I will never know. We might have been able to help prevent monstrous, truly grotesque, acts against humankind. Dear God, I pray we are not too late to save any survivors."

He waved over his head the documents—German and English translations—then read the English versions aloud to the assembly.

GERMAN LANGUAGE TRANSCRIPTION

An J.A. TOPF UND SCHNE
Erfurt, den 8,9,1942
Abteilung D IV
Reichsfuhrer SS, Berlin-Lichterfelde-West.
Krematorium - Auschwitz.

Vertraulich! Geheim!

Herr Obersturmfuhrer Krone ruft an und erklart, dass er zum Brigadefuhrer Kammler bestellt sei under uber seine Besichtigung des Krematoriums in Auschwitz, von der er gestern zuruchkgekehrt sei, zu berichten habe. Aus der Anlage in Auschwitz ware er nicht klug geworden und wollte sich des-halb genau informer, wieviel Muffeln dort zur Zeit in Betrieb seien, under wieviele Ofen mit Muffeln wir zur Zeit dort bauen under noch liefern.

Ich gab an, dass zur Zeit 3 Stuck Zwei-muffel-ofen mit einer Leistung von 250 je Tag in Betrieb seien. Ferner waren jetzt in Bau 5 Stuck Dreimuffel-Ofen mit einer tag lichen Leistung von 800. Zum Versand Kamen heute under in den nachsten Tagen die von Mogilew abgezweigten 2 Stuck Acht-muffel-Ofen mit einer Leistung von je 800 taglich.

Herr K. erklarte, dass diese Anzahl von Muffeln noch nicht aus-reichend sei; wir sollen noch weitere Ofen schnell-stens liefern.

Es ist daher zweckmabig, dass ich am Donnerstag Vor-mittag nach Berlin kame, um mit Herrn K. Uber weitere Lieferungen zu sprechen. Ich soll Unterlagen uber Auschwitz mitbringen, damit nun engulfing einmal die dringenden Rufe vestment wurden.

*

"*Translation*

"*To J.A. TOPF UND SOHNE*
Erfurt, 8,9,1942
Department: D-IV
Reichsfuhrer SS, Berlin-Lichterfelde-West.
Krematorium - Auschwitz-Birkenau.

"*Confidential!*　　　*Secret!*

"*Herr Oberstrumfuhrer Krone calls to say that he was summoned to meet with Brigadefuhrer Kammler and to report on his inspection of the crematorium in Auschwitz, whence he had returned yesterday. He could make nothing of the facilities at Auschwitz and wanted therefore to inform himself on how many muffles are in operation there at this time and how many ovens with muffles we are building there, and at other facilities, and are still to be delivered.*

"*I told him that at this time 3 double-muffle ovens are in operation at Auschwitz-Birkenau, with a capacity of 250 per day. Further, currently under construction are 5 triple muffle ovens with a daily capacity of 800. Today and in the next few days, 2 eight-muffle ovens, each with a daily capacity of 800 will come on consignment, redirected from Mogilew. Each location has differing needs.*

"Mr. K said that this number of muffles is not yet sufficient; we should deliver more ovens as quickly as possible.

"Thus, it is appropriate that I come to Berlin Thursday morning in order to discuss further deliveries with Mr. K. I should bring documents on Auschwitz with me, so that the urgent calls can be finally silenced once and for all."

*

'C' took a big drink of water, plopped down on a wooden chair for a long moment, removed a handkerchief from his jacket and wiped his brow, then slowly unfolded the next document and stood up. No one said a word, Kenny believed the Director was ill. 'C' commenced reading.

"LIST OF NAZI CONCENTRATION CAMPS

In Germany - Poland - Serbia - Norway - Estonia - Netherlands - France - Italy - Belgium - Latvia - Ukraine - Lithuania - Belarus - Austria - Alsace-Lorraine - and Czechoslavakia.

"Specific locations include:

Amersfoort
Arbeitsdorf
Auschwitz-Birkenau

Banjica
Bardufoss
Belzec
Bergen-Belsen
Berlin-Marzahn
Bogdanovka
Bolzano
Bredtvet
Breendonk
Breitenau
Buchenwald
Chelmno
Crveni krst
Dachau
Drancy
Falstad
Flossenburg
Fort de Romainville
Grini
Gross-Rosen
Herzogenbusch
Hinzert
Janowska
Kaiserwald
Kaufering/Landsberg
Kauen, Klooga
Langenstein-Zwieberge
LeVernet
Majdanek
Malchow
Maly Trostenets

Mauthausen-Gusen
Mittelbau-Dora
Natzweiler-Struthof
Neuengamme
Neiderhagen
Ohrdruf
Oranienburg
Osthofen
Plaszow
Ravensbruck
Risiera di San Sabba
Sachsenhausen
Sajmiste
Salaspils
Sobobor
Soldau
Stuthof
Theresienstadt
Treblinka
Vaivara
Warsaw
and Westerbork. "

* * *

Vladimir Kopecky, a 62 year old widower, and member of the Czech Resistance, crouched in the snow-covered, forested hillside overlooking *Theresienstadt*. He resided two miles away, over the bakery that he'd inherited from his parents. Nazis frequented his shop, along with the few remaining locals.

Since 1942 he'd assisted more than two dozen inmate escapes from the death camp, by first hiding one or two at a time in his basement, feeding them for several days, providing available medicine and clothing, then accompanying them, under the cover of darkness, past ever-present Nazi patrols to a second house, fifteen miles North, where he turned them over to another Resistance member or team. From there, dozens of similar transfers occurred, all the way to Sweden—or until the escapees encountered British or American forces. Theirs was a long chain to salvation.

Vladimir Kopecky had interviewed each one of them and sent a written report to Allied authorities. He was warned repeatedly about exaggerating and spreading propaganda. He never learned who made it to safety, and who didn't.

Throughout the freezing November morning and afternoon he watched several thousand inmates—some nearly naked—being herded into boxcars on three 70+ unit trains. He'd intended to make an accurate count, but he stopped after the first hour, choosing instead to scrutinize details about the evacuation.

Much shouting and shoving occurred. No one carried personal belongings or clothing. Twenty-five were shot dead by Nazi guards for moving too slowly, collapsing, attempting to aid another, or fleeing in a panic from the four-abreast queue. Men, women, children, and babies were crowded together. When each boxcar appeared to be completely full, more were squeezed in. Occupants needed to stand erect—unable to move. Screams rang out constantly from family members being forcibly separated from each other.

After each boxcar door was latched shut, rows of faces peered from the air-space slot near the roof. Scrawny arms reached out, as though grasping for help.

A prostitute had informed Vladimir Kopecky the previous night that the trains were heading to a destination in Oswiecim, Poland. The German translation was Auschwitz.

*   *   *

Dear Kenny,

Good news, Sweetheart! I'm headed back to Europe somewhere to set up one of the treatment centers for repatriated prisoners-of-war. I pray to God that they have been well-cared for.

Also, I received a field promotion to Lieutenant Colonel. Atten-hut! Hup hup hup! You can salute me later.

My handwriting is jiggly because I am writing it on the airplane. We're flying through turbulence. The pilot keeps telling us, "No worries." He said he has flown through a lot worse dozens of times. None of us know where we are going, but rumors speculate EVERYWHERE. The Senior Officer asked anybody who wants to write an expedited letter to do so while we are still in the air, so that he can collect them for mailing <u>before</u> we land. That way, none of us can inform dear ones—or even hint about our destination in our letters.

Secrecy - secrecy - secrecy. Oh, how I would like to tell you things, Sweetheart. But, I can't. What if you couldn't tell Cambridge and Oxford University deans even where you are? What if your students could only guess what classroom to go to for your next lecture or physics lab?

After all, we are winning the war now! We keep getting updates about victories in the other theaters. Against the Japs, too. Hooray!! I certainly understand why secrecy is necessary. The location of my unit could never be disclosed for obvious reasons—or the whereabouts of General Montgomery's tanks. He always seemed to know where Rommel kept his, though. Amazing, huh? I don't see how he always managed to do it. Brits picked the right man for the job.

During a 25 day period some time ago, we moved the hospital three times. Not because we were under attack. Quite the opposite. General Montgomery had all his tanks and army chasing Rommel and <u>his</u> tanks. All along the way we saw blown up and undamaged Panzer tanks that had simply run out of gas. Our caseload tripled due to treating severely-injured German prisoners in great numbers. Mobile operating rooms were set up in the back of several trucks for the most serious cases. We pulled 20 hour daily shifts umpteen days in a row.

Last night, those of us being re-assigned had a going-away party with staff, rear-guard Command, available troops, and ambulatory Allied patients.

I see the day coming very very soon, Sweetheart, when you will always know where I am. I won't be required by the Army or anybody else to keep secrets from you anymore. I'll be right by your side. You will see. Gotta go!

Love as ever,

Teddy

P.S. - I thank the Lord every day that you haven't gotten involved in this horrific war.

*

U.S. EMBASSY
LONDON

Dear Jane,

My little sister has done it again!

I've been hearing great things about your USO tour! Praise from military leaders and elected officials has been what you and your show business friends would call *boffo*. Winston Churchill even

sent an appreciative note about you and Marlene Dietrich to the Ambassador, who personally
showed it to me. Everybody here knows we are
related. The Prime Minister expressed his desire
to attend a performance by your troupe in London when it can be safely scheduled. The way the
war is going, we expect that to be sooner than
later.

I am so very proud of you, Jane. Your com-
mitment to the USO entertainment program,
and the important role you have played boost-
ing troop morale throughout the war has been a
Godsend. I confess. I've laid awake nights when
I learned how close you are to the front lines at
many of your stops. God is on our side!

Love and kisses from your proud stepbrother,

George

Maj. George Fisher

P.S. - I'm on the promotion list.

Chapter Twenty-five

U.S. Army Major Glenn Blakely stared at Auschwitz-Birkenau concentration camp from his open tank hatch, as he rolled toward the entrance. His was the lead tank of the 11th Armored Division. Unmanned watchtowers—spaced every fifty yards—surrounded the site. Skeleton-like humans peered through the ten-foot high, barbed-wire fence that many prisoners leaned against for support. Overhead, the gate sign read, "Arbeit, Macht, Frei." German-speaking Sergeant Luke Brandt, standing beside the Major, interpreted it as, "Labor will free you."

"Hell is paradise compared to what we are about to discover," replied the Major.

Seemingly endless rows of long, narrow, ghetto-like, wooden barracks lined the left side of the wide entryway that led to a one-level, brick building, containing a one hundred-foot high, eight-foot wide smokestack—the *Crematorium*. He'd heard about the *ovens*, but hadn't believed the stories until recently.

The spacious courtyard just inside the gate contained five gallows and three whipping posts. Stacked high in multiple piles were decomposing bodies, whose stench could be detected from several miles away. Various-sized sheds, without signs, stood everywhere.

One hundred yards to the right was what appeared to be a two-story headquarters building with a balcony that overlooked the courtyard. Behind it was a metal building. Atop its roof, a sign read, *Bathing and Showers*.

Beyond the *Crematorium*, a railroad siding contained dozens of locked boxcars.

Early that morning Major Blakely was briefed that he might face token resistance from remaining Nazis, but there'd been none. They'd fled with most of the prisoners—leaving more than two thousand behind.

As the tanks and soldiers entered the courtyard, prisoners appeared at barracks doorways and windows. Some cheered. Four drunk Nazi soldiers in soiled uniforms emerged from the Headquarters Building and staggered forward, holding their hands high in the air. One waved a white flag.

"We ask for asylum," shouted one, in broken English.

"I will only accept surrender," replied Major Blakely.

Sergeant Brandt interpreted. The four nodded.

"Are there more of you?" asked the Major.

The Nazis shook their heads.

"Where are the other prisoners?" asked the Major.

"They began a thirty mile march to Wodzislaw five days ago. From there ... Buchenwald... when trains become available."

"How many prisoners departed from here?"

The Nazi shrugged. "Ten thousand?"

* * *

Intercepts flooded into Bletchley Park during the final throes of Nazi aggression, particularly in the Ardennes during the *Battle of the Bulge*. Some originated directly from Hitler's underground bunker. Many were frantic messages between ragtag Nazi units, retreating, hiding, disguising, destroying and burying evidence of criminal wrongdoing, and evacuating the plethora of concentration camps. In their haste and panic, Nazi radio operators and encrypters reverted to simple codes—even plain language—in the absence of Enigma machines they'd left behind.

'C' constantly reminded staffers that "Hitler would be mortified to learn we are aware of his plans, ahead of his own field commanders."

It was evident to everyone at Bletchley Park there were other death camps equal to the horrors and numbers of murders as Auschwitz-Birkenau. Included were Bergen-Belsen, Buchenwald, Dachau, Flossenburg, Gross-Rosen, Maulhausen, Ohrdruf, Sachsenhausen, Sobodor, and Treblinka.

Kenny discovered that the '*Bathing and Showers*' sign was synonymous with '*Homicidal Gas Chambers Disguised as Showers*'. '*Special Treatment (Sonderbehandlung)*' meant, '*Immediate Gassing of All, Upon Arrival*'. The locked boxcars found at Auschwitz-Birkenau contained dead Jews awaiting *final transfer* to the Crematorium ovens.

Alastair Denniston informed 'C', Kenny, and Alan Turing that he didn't want to speculate which others on the *List of Nazi Concentration Camps* were similarly-supplied.

"We'll let the liberators tell us," he said.

Detailed reports didn't stop. Some decrypters and cryptanalysts fainted at their work stations.

* * *

Field Hospital in Northern England

The Army surgeon whispered to Teddy that the next malnourished patient had a fractured clavicle and pelvis, ulcerated lacerations in his back from whippings, broken ribs and jaw, pervasive bruise trauma, and a lacerated liver.

"It's a miracle this one survived the *death march*," he said. His brethren needed to hold him upright. He managed to stay ambulatory. They saved his life."

It was Teddy's fifteenth straight hour of surgery. She'd lost count of how many operations she'd assisted during her shift, as one of several dozen surgical nurses. Ten surgeries occurred simultaneously for days on end. Relief was available by simply nodding her head, but she chose not to. Triage nurses and medics constantly shouted symptoms and vital signs about those next in the queue—along with noisy, but organized, preps for the "next case." Surgeons stepped to other operating tables occasionally, depending on their particular specialty—if any. Everybody assisted everyone.

Teddy had been informed that during the previous seventy-two hours, more than seven thousand liberated prisoners had been delivered to dozens of Field Hospitals. Countless numbers died in transit. Many were not expected to survive medical or surgical treatment.

"First, we'll repair the liver," said the surgeon.

The patient breathed heavily through the ether cup, held in place by the anesthetist. Teddy noticed that the patient was bald. Not even eyebrows. That's what drew her attention to him. His skin showed traces of makeup. A tingly vibration surged through her body. She gripped the edge of the operating table and stared. She'd seen the man before. In another place. Recognition jolted her brain. She lowered her face close to the patient's to be certain.

"Take a break," said the surgeon.

"Klaus?" she screamed.

"Do you know this patient?"

"Klaus… this is Klaus… this is Klaus Leonhardt! Klaus… we found you!"

Chapter Twenty-six

With great anticipation and anxiety, Jane waited outside the huge, post-op tent. Marlene Dietrich sat beside her, holding her hand. The two had been flown from the USO Tour to the Field Hospital, immediately after they'd been informed about Klaus. Only fourteen hours had elapsed since his operation.

The cable from Teddy contained a candid, frightening description of his condition and appearance. Jane yearned to be near him—alternately crying and laughing joyfully about the prospect.

The Jeep ride from the air strip shocked her. The scene was far worse than she'd imagined. Hundreds of recently-rescued evacuees—resembling skin-coated skeletons, clothed in baggy rags—were lined up on gurneys, lying on the ground on blankets, in the back of ambulances, and medic-borne stretchers. Some were dead. It was hard to tell. Military chaplains were everywhere.

Teddy appeared out of nowhere, hugged both women consolingly, and led them into the facility.

Long rows of occupied beds and cots came into view. Ether and disinfectants permeated the air. Wide-awake patients stared vacantly through sunken eye sockets—even if they were sitting up. Some mumbled incoherently, and pointed at them with their frail, bony fingers. Nurses and medics hovered over many. Teddy stopped at Klaus's bed.

"Klaus isn't aware of your visit," she whispered. "He's heavily sedated… hasn't awakened since surgery."

An oxygen tent covered his upper body. Tubes jutted out. One leg was in a cast. Jane stared at his sunken eyes and cheeks, grasped his hand, and wept.

"His recovery will take some time," whispered Teddy. "Possibly, several months. He's being sent to a military hospital in London."

"When he awakens, tell him that I love him and miss him and will always take care of him. We're getting married, you know," said Jane.

"I expect Klaus to be in a picture with you by next year," said Marlene Dietrich.

"Yes… yes, the three of us together."

"Jane, talk like that will have him leaping right out of bed and grabbing you," said Teddy.

"Are these other patients liberated prisoners-of-war?" asked Jane.

"Jews… all of them," replied Marlene.

"Hitler is exterminating entire families… three or four generations back," said Teddy. "Other prisoners protected Klaus… even shaved his head and applied makeup to obscure his identity."

"But, why Klaus?" asked Jane. "He starred in *Liebesraum* for Germany … and narrated a documentary film about *Theresein-stadt*. Children were singing. So many people. I don't understand. What happened to all of *them*?"

"Dead," replied Teddy. "We've been told that the Nazis were saving Klaus until last, so that he would suffer the most… knowing how they died. Hitler hates successful Jews."

"I still don't understand," said Jane. "Klaus isn't Jewish."

"His grandmother was," said Marlene.

* * *

Reports of Klaus Leonhardt's rescue circled the globe. Nazi atrocities at concentration camps were becoming well-publicized.

Following an inspection of *Buchenwald*, General George Patton ordered every resident of the nearby town, Weimar, Germany, to see it for themselves, "so they know what they've been living next to for years... and can't pretend they haven't." The townspeople were marched together to the concentration camp. Weimar's mayor and his wife, who'd frequently entertained the Camp Commandant and his lieutenants at their home, committed suicide the next day.

General Dwight D. Eisenhower, likewise, ordered all local residents near *Auschwitz-Birkenau* to the concentration camp— subsequent to his grisly visit there with General Omar Bradley— "to prevent future propagandists from altering history." Journalists and photographers attended, en masse.

Edward R. Murrow, during a radio broadcast, reported "rows of bodies stacked up like cordwood. If I've offended you by this rather mild account of *Buchenwald*, I'm not in the least sorry. For most of it, I have no words."

"We are in the presence of a crime without a name," stated Winston Churchill, in an address to Parliament.

* * *

April 12, 1945
Washington, D.C.

PRESIDENT ROOSEVELT DEAD
HARRY TRUMAN SWORN-IN AS U.S. PRESIDENT

*   *   *

April 30, 1945

Kenny stared at the most current intercept from Hitler's Berlin bunker in disbelief. He had a limited German vocabulary, but he knew the translation for the word—*tot*. It simply meant, *dead*. He showed it to Alan Turing.

They alerted Alastair Denniston, and the three rushed past Mrs. Pemberton into 'C's office.

It read in part: DER FUEHRER ADOLF HITLER IST TOT.

The mass murderer had committed suicide.

Within minutes, every corridor and office in the mansion, Huts, and other out-buildings at Bletchley Park were alive with cheers, hugging, and prolonged celebrations.

*   *   *

May 7, 1945

GERMANY SURRENDERS!

Chapter Twenty-seven

Kenny's work was finished at Bletchley Park. 'C' reduced the rent on the Teddington house to zero—until Teddy was discharged from the Royal Army three months later. The Kroneldts returned to America and resumed their former positions at the University of Nebraska and Lincoln General Hospital.

Jane toured with the USO Troupe throughout Europe until shortly after the Japanese surrendered in August. Klaus showed significant improvement at each of her frequent visits in London. They sailed to America just before Christmas, 1945, and planned a Hollywood wedding.

Bletchley Park ceased operations. The machinery was dismantled to maintain secrecy. 'C' and Alastair Denniston returned to their old offices in London.

* * *

"How can there be so much talent in one family," said Alastair Denniston. "Professor Kroneldt and Jane Palmer were brought up as orphans, for God's sake!"

"A brother and sister act... worthy of some notice," replied 'C'. "I'm taking the Lancia for a spin. Care to go?"